THE SMOKER'S HANDBOOK

Survival Guide for a Dying Breed

Conor Goodman

NEW ISLAND

**To my chain-smoking wife, Niamh.
May you never give up on me.**

THE SMOKER'S HANDBOOK
Survival Guide for a Dying Breed
First published November 2001
by New Island Books
2 Brookside
Dundrum Road
Dublin 14

Copyright © Conor Goodman, 2001

ISBN 1 902602 76 5

All rights reserved. The material in this publication is protected by copyright law. Except as may be permitted by law, no part of the material may be reproduced (including by storage in a retrieval system) or transmitted in any form or by any means; adapted; rented or lent without the written permission of the copyright owners. Applications for permission should be addressed to the publisher.

British Library Cataloguing in Publication Data
A catalogue record for this book is available from the British Library.

New Island received financial assistance from The Arts Council
(An Chomhairle Ealaíon), Dublin, Ireland.

Cover design: Jon Berkeley
Interior illustrations: Michael McCarthy
Printed in Ireland by Colour Books Ltd.

Contents

INTRODUCTION 6

1. ENDING IT ALL: Quitting Smoking 9
2. WHAT ARE WE LIKE?: The smoker's personality 27
3. YOU-NAME-IT, SMOKING CAN SERIOUSLY DAMAGE IT: The smoker's body 35
4. NOWHERE LEFT TO GO: The smoker's space 51
5. WHO IS 'BIG TOBACCO'?: The tobacco industry 65
6. A LAND CALLED SUE: Courtroom drama 71
7. THE WORLD IS YOUR SMOKING ROOM: The smoker's planet 83
8. COUGHING UP FOR YOUR COUNTRY: The price of smoking 101
9. PUBLICITY WARS: Selling cigarettes 113
10. SMOKERS – THE PREMIER LEAGUE: Target marketing 129
11. YOU SAY TOMATO, I SAY TOBACCO: The smoker's choices 143

The rise of smoking

- **1 BC** Native Americans begin using tobacco in religious and medicinal practices.
- **1492** Columbus sails ocean blue. Natives give him tobacco as a gift. Bemused, he throws it away.
- **1556** Tobacco reaches Europe.
- **1571** Spanish doctor Nicolas Monardes claims tobacco can cure 36 bodily ills.
- **1586** Walter Raleigh learns how to smoke a pipe.
- **1604** King James I writes *A Counterblaste to Tobacco*.
- **1612** John Rolfe harvests Virginia's first successful tobacco crop, making the colony economically viable for the first time.
- **1665** Smoking thought to protect against Black Death.
- **1847** Philip Morris founded.
- **1852** Matches introduced.
- **1856** Soldiers bring cigarettes back to England from the Crimean War.
- **1863** Gallaher Tobacco founded in Belfast.
- **1875** RJ Reynolds founded.
- **1880** First cigarette machine patented.
- **1902** British American Tobacco founded.
- **1913** Camel launched.

1914-18 Cigarettes given free to soldiers in World War I. A generation is addicted.

1920 Cigarette most popular tobacco product in UK.

1927 Lucky Strike ads target women.

1932 Zippo lighter invented.

1939-45 During World War II, smoking hits an all-time high.

1948 Lung cancer now most common form of the disease.

1950 First major study linking smoking and lung cancer.

1954 Winston, the first commercially successful filter brand, is launched.

1964 US surgeon general's report *Smoking and Health* officially identifies smoking as a health hazard.

1965 Cigarette ads taken off British TV.

1968 Lotus is first Formula 1 team to be sponsored by a tobacco brand, John Player.

1971 Health warning printed on UK cigarette boxes.

1988 In USA, first successful liability suit against a tobacco company. $400,000 award later overturned. World No-Tobacco Day inaugurated.

1992 *Cigar Aficionado* magazine is launched.

1995 Internal tobacco industry papers go on the Internet.

1998 US tobacco firms agree to pay $205 billion to have lawsuits by states dropped.

2001 Philip Morris ordered to pay $100 million to cancer victim Richard Boeken. Further appeals refused.

I quit (every half hour or so)

INTRODUCTION

Just a few years ago, it looked like the world was giving up smoking. The once-mighty tobacco industry was besieged by lawsuits and faced declining ad and sales opportunities. Smokers were being hounded from cinemas, office blocks and even the odd pub, and bombarded with props to help them kick the habit: hypnosis, funny-tasting gum and bizarre little inhalers shaped "just like a cigarette".

For starters, you're saved the bother of having to defend the indefensible. I mean, smoking as we know it has ceased to make sense. It's bad for your health, it's impossible to find a place to light up in peace, and you practically need to take out a mortgage just to buy a box of fags.

As well as avoiding the general harassment that smokers are subjected to, quitters can smoke as much as they like. Failure to quit is not just accepted; it's expected.

According to the modern interpretation of smoking, we are not to blame for our habit. Smokers are the puppets of global corporations who have brainwashed us with advertising, hooked us with nicotine, and secured our addiction with chemical additives. Against these forces, how could we succeed?

It's hardly surprising, then, that everybody I know seems to be in one state or another of quitting, relapse, smoking on the sly or rolling ten joints a day. Perhaps it's all these "serial quitters" who are keeping the habit alive. Because, against all the odds, smoking refuses to die.

The habit could have become a footnote to the history of the 20th century. Instead, everybody went cigar-crazy, the tobacco industry bought off the litigants, and smoking in Ireland and Britain began to creep up again, after decades in steady decline.

So what made me decide to write a book on the subject? I believe most of the information that reaches the public about smoking is propaganda — for either the tobacco industry or the anti-smoking lobby. I have tried to sift through this whirl of statistics and information, and address the topics that interest me as a smoker — or at least as a regular stopper. I hope that, for those curious about their habit and its current place in the world, this book may serve as a primer in the mysteries of smoking.

Conor Goodman, 2001

1 *Ending it all*
QUITTING SMOKING

"Those who give up smoking aren't the heroes. The real heroes are the rest of us who have to listen to them." **Hal Boyle**

Sooner or later, we all get there: that sneezing, sniffing, coughing, blood-spitting, lung-aching, foul-smelling, ashen-faced, inhaler-snorting, nauseous, powerless and worthless state that makes us cry "enough". "No more shall I be a slave to this vice. No more of the decrepit wrinkly who stared out of the bathroom mirror this morning. Today, I file for divorce from cigarettes."

Good for you. It's a tough decision. Well actually, it's an easy-peasy decision, just a tough one to commit to for more than about five hours. So take a deep breath. If you can't manage that, bracing yourself or girding your loins will do just as well. Warn your nearest and dearest. Bid your friends farewell. Maybe make a brief home-video of "the old you". Life is about to get weird.

Stage 1: The one-track mind
Upon giving up smoking, it quickly becomes apparent that you've just swapped one miserable lifestyle for another. Overnight, cigarettes

become the most ubiquitous commodity on the planet. People who barely acknowledged your existence before seem to be offering you a fag every ten minutes, and long cylindrical objects are suddenly deeply significant.

Cigarettes gnaw at your brain and consume your thoughts. Male, are you? Used to think 60 times a day about sex? Consider yourself cured (temporarily anyway). Women who scour magazines for features on Gucci bags and Prada shoes now see only photo after photo of skinny, happy, chain-smoking models. It seems that since you quit smoking, the world has taken it up.

And what brilliant conversationalists all smokers are. How relaxed, witty and generally masterful at social events, where you, virtually dumbstruck, resort to mumbling earnestly about shattered nerves, overpowering cravings and how you used to smoke like a synthetic armchair. "Hey, I was on 30 a day, no 35, more than you anyway. Really, I'm cool too."

And you know everything would be all right if you could only have one itty bitty ciggy.

Stage 2: Coping

Still determined, you make a few practical rules to help cope with this new-found inadequacy.

● Beware relapse flashpoints, like the moments immediately after a good meal. Many an attempt to quit has foundered on the rocks of a post-prandial scotch. Solution: don't eat, or if you eat, don't stop.

- Remove temptations by destroying all cigarettes in the house. If there are other smokers in the house, destroy them too, and if there is a shop nearby where you can buy cigarettes, move house to a more remote location. Moving house is highly stressful, so it may be easier on your quitting regime to simply burn the shop — and don't even think about standing nearby to inhale the fumes.
- To cheer your poor little cigaretteless self up, put all the money you normally spend on cigarettes into a little jar and watch it pile up. If you can manage this you will have succeeded in turning your perfectly nice, spontaneous self — whose normal impulse is probably to take money out of jars, whether it's yours or not, and spend it in the pub — into an uptight miser.

Stage 3: Fascism

After a couple of weeks, you realise the easiest way to kill the pain is to become one yourself. You are on the slow road to personality death — similar to brain death, but more stressful for friends and relatives.

Bereft of any personal characteristics, the brain's normal reaction is to devote itself wholly to bodily longevity. The erstwhile habit of smoking is replaced by the more noble pursuit of jogging. The after-dinner cigarette is substituted by a brisk walk to aid digestion. The post-coital one is accounted for by the denial of coitus by your partner, who at this point is having death fantasies about you.

Who cares? You're too busy jogging vertically to be interested in the horizontal variety. And besides, you've probably fallen in love with that wonderful person who has not admitted any nicotine to either side of their perfect brain for two weeks.

Inevitably, your attitude towards your old cronies changes. Your new approach generally consists of affecting a coughing fit when somebody lights a cigarette in your presence, dishing out Shocking Statistics About Smoking, emptying ashtrays which people are obviously using, and jawing on about how absolutely tip-top you feel since you gave up those loathsome things.

Your diet turns odd too. Coffee goes down the drain, along with your few remaining friendships. Rock-like, you resist alcohol, avoid salt, and muse that it's probably just as well that you no longer have any friends, because it's looking increasingly likely that you're going to outlive them all anyway. Indeed, it can't be ruled out that you might live forever.

Stage ultimate: relapse

That could be as good as it gets: a long life that seems even longer without your favourite poison. But the fact is, urges can occur at the most inopportune moments — hours, days or even years after you've quit. They become less frequent but never quite pass.

Above all, take heart if you don't succeed. The road to self-improvement is littered with potholes, and nearly all those who try to quit come a cropper sooner or later (but usually sooner). Most people who successfully quit have at least three or four failed attempts behind them, and failure has its little compensations: you'll be happy for about five minutes before you start despising yourself again; other people will stop hating you; and you can comfort yourself with that incontrovertible smoker's logic that, even if you gave up today, you could always be knocked over by a bus tomorrow.

Chances of success

Before embarking on the painful journey that quitting smoking entails, you should have some idea of your chances of success. The medics who study this kind of thing don't exactly produce bookies' odds, but here are some of the factors that increase or decrease your chances of successfully giving up.

First there's the amount you smoke. Very light or occasional smokers cough, wheeze and ache less than 40-a-dayers and are in relative control of their cigarette intake, so they don't feel the same need to give up. Heavy smokers have more to gain from quitting, and so are more motivated. Motivation is big.

The number of years you've smoked is important too. A long-term habit is actually a good indicator of success for someone trying to quit. Teenagers, for example, don't have the same sense of immediacy, believing that they have plenty of time to give up.

Then there's the manner in which you smoke. People who suck in a lot of nicotine per cigarette are seen as "more addicted" than light suckers, and tend to go back on the fags quite easily.

And people who have been made sick by cigarettes are less likely than those with a clean bill of health to give up for keeps. Half the smokers who have operations for lung cancer go back on cigarettes afterwards. Among heart attack victims the relapse rate is 70%.

Your home life obviously makes a difference. People who live with a non-smoking adult and child are six times more likely to quit than those who live alone.

These are some of the pre-existing conditions that affect a quitter's success rate. But they are far less important than the behaviour you adopt when you give up.

Quitters who give in to temptation within the first 24 hours — even take a drag from a friend — have essentially dashed their chances of giving up, and revert to their normal rate of consumption within six months. (A bit earlier, I'd say. Within a week they are probably taking inch-long drags of their pals' cigarettes, within two they're forgetting to give them back, and in three weeks they are either buying their own or looking for new friends.) The team who discovered this concluded that people who smoke on "quit day" might as well resume smoking immediately, and work towards giving up again at a future date.

Getting through the first day smoke-free shows you're serious and actually increases your chances tenfold. But smokers find it hard to

They ain't heavy — or are they? Myth of the light cigarette

Are you a low-Tarzan? A Holly Smoke-Lightly? Most smokers now choose brands described as "light" or "low-tar" — an ingenious label which convinces us poor buggers that we're doing ourselves some good when in fact we're just postponing the day when we have to quit.

Light cigarettes should be less harmful, given their lower concentrations of tar and of nicotine, and they could be too if we only knew how to smoke them. But the light cigarette is every bit as bad for us as its fuller-bodied counterpart, all as a result of the smoker's ineptitude.

I had always thought that smoking was about lighting up, then sucking, then posing, then exhaling. However, things are more complicated for the smoker of lights. Light cigarettes are created by the manufacturer making tiny holes in the filter of a normal cigarette. The theory is that these perforations reduce the draw on the tobacco part of the cigarette so that less smoke enters the mouth.

But we smokers unknowingly do everything possible to counter these precautions. For starters, we cover the holes with our fingers. Then we wet the filter with our lips, closing up more perforations. Finally, to compensate for any remaining gaps between our cigarettes and the non-light variety, we take massive inward snorts.

The vigorous puffing makes light cigarette smokers every bit as likely to get lung cancer as their seemingly more carefree pals. The EU intends to ban the words "light" and "mild" from cigarette packets by 2003.

play the self-disciplinarian for long. Even the most vigilant tend after a few days, weeks or months to drop their guard, adopt an oh-what-a-good-ex-smoker-am-I attitude, and have a fag. One, just one, cigarette taken in a split second of weakness is enough to re-establish your habit to its former glory in a matter of days.

One study found that the second week off cigarettes is crucial too. A group of people stopped smoking, and their progress was checked after two weeks and again after six months. Most people who smoked in the second week had resumed smoking within six months.

Finally, there's the C-word. Most medical advisers agree that commitment to giving up is probably the most important factor.

Getting fatter

22% of women and 34% of men are ex-smokers, so it's possible to quit, but it's no cake-walk. About a quarter of all smokers try to stop every year, but the most encouraging statistic I have been able to find is that just 4% make it (the worst said 0.2%). For those using nicotine replacement or other aids, the success rates rise to 10%-30%, though some of these are the results of trials run by the drug companies, and I can't help taking them with a pinch of snuff.

At this point I have tried most of the products and quit therapies on the market: nicotine-releasing chewing gum, skin patches, spray that you stick up your nose, even hypnosis. I found most of the products either unergonomic or just plain disgusting to taste, but they make your slim chances slightly fatter.

Tampon-chewing ... and ten other ways to stop smoking

I should point out that these methods might work for you even though they failed for me. But they aren't worth trying unless you really want to give up. Even if you do, I've found that's no guarantee either ...

Chewing gum: Quitting smoking is bad enough without putting yourself through this further sensory torture. The reason quitting aids all sound like they are called knicker-something is that they taste like old underpants, and nicotine chewing gum is the grossest of the lot. Those taste buds you thought you'd killed will be raised from the dead by its vile tang. Apart from that, chewing gum is impractical if you're out for a pint. It goes badly with booze. But then, don't we all. Having said that, it sticks well to the undersides of tables.
The Damage: Around £15 for a week's supply.

The patch: My short-sighted loved one thought I had sprouted a third nipple, but on smokeless nights I'm more at ease if I have a patch on. The person who introduced me to them insisted that smoking while wearing a patch would lead to nicotine poisoning and violent nausea. It doesn't, I discovered eventually. *The Damage: Around £15 for a week's supply (20mg patches cost roughly the same as 10mg and 5mg ones. I'm still trying to work out if you can buy 20mg ones and halve/quarter them).*

Nicotine inhaler: Hello. My name's Conor, and I've got a tampon in my mouth. That's not just how it looks, it's how it tastes too.
The Damage: Around £6 for starter pack with six cartridges (it's recommended you use not more than 12 a day).

Hypnosis: I did not emerge from the session convinced that I had never smoked, nor that the habit was repulsive, nor that all the people around me were naked dwarfs. But I first attended in mid-December and made it as far as New Year's Eve before caving in. The first hour of the session consisted of a psychoanalysis of my habit, and the second half I spent in a doze-like state, listening to dreamy music as the hypnotist asked me to picture myself as a non-smoker five years thence. If nothing else, the shrink-style preliminaries gave me a good understanding of my real reasons for smoking and — if I may slip into buzzwordery for a moment — it was the most "empowering" therapy I have tried. And don't presume, as I did, that you're too independent-minded for hypnosis. Smokers, as a rule, do not have wills of iron, and you're probably as receptive as the next person to having your subconscious recalibrated. *The Damage: £120 for two two-hour sessions.*

Acupuncture: Medical literature doesn't rate acupuncture highly as a quitting aid, but then it doesn't rate smoking very highly as a practice. The central thrust of this therapy is to combat withdrawal symptoms. Nicotine stimulates the release of endorphins in the brain, but their levels fall when you quit. Acupuncture, by applying needles to certain pressure points around the neck and ear, helps stimulate this process again, so the quitting smoker is less of a bag of nerves. It also claims to address appetite cravings and stress levels. ***The Damage:** Around £150 for a full programme.*

Laser therapy: Luke Skywalker belts you on the head with a light sabre until you stop smoking. That could work actually, but in fact the approach is more Yoda-like. Using the same principles as acupuncture (but no needles), laser therapy helps you behave like a relatively normal human being while you're engaged in Tar Wars. The best thing about these new-age therapists is they don't just send you off to the chemist with a prescription, but take a personalised approach, asking smokers at length about their habit and often supplementing the therapy with herbal remedies. ***The Damage:** Around £150 for a course of therapy (two to three sessions).*

Zyban: Originally prescribed to traumatised Vietnam veterans as an anti-depressant, Zyban was found to have several side-effects, among them diminished nicotine cravings. Others include sleeplessness (boooh!), dry mouth (big deal) and diminished appetite (whoopee! And speaking of whoopee, it can make you fart too, although nobody tells you that). Zyban is unusual for two reasons. First, unlike other pharmacological solutions, it contains no nicotine, so some people try it in conjunction with gum or patches for extra effect. Second, users continue smoking for their first week or two on the drug, so if you're bothered by the immediacy of quitting then this priming period might help. However, sales dropped in 2001, following the death of a 21-year-old flight attendant after taking Zyban in conjunction with the anti-malarial drug, chloroquine. Thirty-five patients in Britain have died after taking Zyban, although it has not been proven that the drug was the cause of any of these deaths. ***The Damage:*** *Around £125 per month from an Internet supplier (course lasts six to seven weeks). Doctors' advice strongly recommended.*

St John's wort: I haven't tried this as it's still under research, but a study in the University of London suggests this herbal remedy can rebalance the brain's dopamine levels, which fall when smokers quit. If that kind of thing floats your boat then it might be worth a try. Incidentally, it's illegal to sell St John's wort in Ireland (but you can flog cigarettes in any corner shop). ***The Damage:*** *Kira One-A-Day St John's Wort costs around £15 for a pack of 30 in the UK.*

The new nicotine empire

Over the past 10 years, chemists' shops have been flooded with all sorts of fancy gadgets for us poor addicts to splash out on: chewing gum, nicotine patches, nasal spray, the inhalator, the microtab. British smokers (or ex-smokers, or temporary non-smokers) spent £38 million on quitting products in 1998 and are expected to up this to £59 million in 2002.

The secret weapon in this pharmacological armoury is a nicotine vaccine. Clinical trials began in September 2001 on a vaccine which blocks the passage of nicotine to the brain. Unlike users of existing methods, which aim to moderate the withdrawal symptoms from cigarettes, vaccinated quitters will have to go cold turkey. In effect, they have no choice: once you're vaccinated, withdrawal symptoms will not be relieved by smoking. Get your chequebook ready.

Helpline: You're in the pub, someone is talking to you but you're far away in nicotine fantasy-land, thinking of how much better life would be if you had just one smoke. Fight it. Ring the number on that little card you picked up in the chemist. Dring, dring. "Thank you for calling the stop-smoking helpline. Our operator is currently talking down another desperate soul. Please hold, and we will take your call as soon as possible." Sod this, I'm having a fag.
The Damage: *Most helplines are free.*

Allen Carr: *Allen Carr's Easy Way to Stop Smoking* has been a best-seller in 20 languages and has clearly found a willing readership among those desperate to kick the habit. Somebody passed me a "lucky" copy around four years ago — everybody who read it had successfully quit, and one of them is still smoke-free — but the only thing I gave up on was Carr's prose. His basic principle ("Giving up smoking is no big deal. The idea that it is is part of the brainwashing.") is novel and may be true, but his 100 ways of writing the same sentence grate after a while. You may be better served by one of Carr's quit-smoking clinics, at which smoking is permitted in the initial stages. If you want to read one of his several titles, *The Little Book of Quitting* is the shortest, cheapest and most portable.

The Damage: *The Little Book of Quitting costs £2.50 from www.amazon.co.uk. www.allencarrseasyway.com is Carr's (slow) website, with details of his books and clinics, and an online quit guide.*

Decapitation: This highly effective method was adopted in the 17th century by an Ottoman sultan, Murad the Cruel, who had all smokers beheaded. Success rate: 100%. ***The Damage:*** *Considerable.*

Some famous smokers who, for one reason or another, are mostly dead

Bob Marley RIP 1945-1981
When Bob Marley smoked, he rolled his own, so to speak, and used only the best local Jamaican ingredients. Millions today follow his example, often with his music as a backdrop, but the difference between them and Marley is that he smoked marijuana as a Rastafarian sacrament — not just to get stoned. In fact, Rastafarianism forbids the use of alcohol and tobacco — indispensable features of most modern weed-smoking sessions — on the grounds that they defile the body. The creed didn't do much for Marley, who died of lung, liver and brain cancer in 1981.

George Burns RIP 1896-1996
US comedian George Burns was a life-long cigar smoker who died aged 100. Burns won an Oscar at 80, played concerts well into his 90s, and in his final years delighted in lighting up at an LA country club where a notice read: "Cigar Smoking Prohibited For Anyone Over 95." He was still smoking 10-15 a day.

John Wayne RIP 1907-1977

Contrast John Wayne's indestructible-hero image with a death from lung cancer and you have a potent anti-smoking message: "If it can kill John Wayne, it sure as hell can kill you." But while he is often cited as an example of the damage smoking can do, Wayne was not in fact a victim of lung cancer. He probably should have been, as a 120-a-day smoker, but he survived the removal of a tumour from his left lung in 1964, only to eventually die of stomach cancer in 1977. Smoking was almost definitely to blame for his lung problems, but the stomach cancer may have had other causes.

A decade before his lung operation, John Wayne played the role of Genghis Khan in *The Conqueror* — not one of his better efforts. The film was shot near a nuclear test site in Utah, where 11 atomic bombs had been exploded the previous year. Cast and crew worked all summer amid radioactive dust and other debris. Of the 220 people working on the film, 91 developed cancer later in life — a figure three times above normal.

2 What are we like?
THE SMOKER'S PERSONALITY

"If we didn't smoke, there'd be precious little going for either of us ... After all, we have no hobbies, outside interests, no hidden accomplishments, and God knows we're not all that nice."
Barbara Ellen, writing in The Observer

It's not easy to say what kind of person smokes. Obviously, all sorts do — young and old, fat and thin, sick and (believe it or not) healthy. But in all their variety, surely there are common threads. I have chosen nearly all my friends and associates from the 30% of the population that smoke cigarettes. Is our only bond that we ignite and inhale leaves rolled in paper? Clearly there's some comfort in that shared ritual, but it's not enough to make us friends for life.

There's a small body of scientific and social literature devoted to the question of what in our personalities makes us smoke and draws smokers together as soul-mates. To sum up the research in a sentence, I would conclude that smokers are unreliable, thrill-seeking, sex-mad, drug-taking, schizophrenics. But to give it a scientific gloss, I should add, "more so than our non-smoking counterparts".

That's how personality is measured in psychology: by degrees, by tendencies towards certain behaviours, by being more likely than not to do something, by greater percentages of people acting one way than the other. The only way to discover what smokers are like is to compare them to non-smokers and show how most of us are different from most of them.

Sensation-seekers

Most smokers are hooked by the age of 16, so our personalities at that age are crucial to whether we become long-termers or not. Studies in the UK have shown that the teenagers drawn to smoking score highly on a measure called the sensation-seeking scale.

This measures one's proclivity for thrill-seeking (sport, and risky or mildly frightening activities), experience-seeking (novel experiences through music, art, travel and other bohemian pursuits), disinhibition (sensation from illegal or unconventional activities), and boredom susceptibility. Those who score low on this scale almost never smoke.

Other factors that draw adolescents to smoking are: low expectation of academic success; poor self-esteem; hopelessness; a greater orientation towards friends than family; and having friends who engage in "problem behaviours".

Later in life, new situations arise for the same people. Divorcees, it turns out, go through more cigarettes than married or single people. People involved in road accidents are more likely to be smokers than not. And those with poor academic records smoke more than straight-A students.

The psychologist, HJ Eysenck, points out that all these behaviours are characteristic of extroversion. In psychological terms, extroverts are not so much people who are good at dinner parties as people with a "stimulus hunger".

This need draws them not just to nicotine, but also to coffee and alcohol, spicy food, premarital and extramarital sex, and generally risky and impulsive behaviour. It's not surprising that those who become addicted to nicotine also have a predisposition to harder drugs, including crack cocaine and glue sniffing. Committed "novelty

The smoker and the shrink

- There's a strong link between smoking and depression. A US study has found 6.6% of smokers are depressed, as against 2.9% of non-smokers.
- Depressives find it twice as hard to give up.
- Smokers are twice as likely as non-smokers to attempt suicide.
- The incidence of smoking among schizophrenics ranges from 75% to 90%, across numerous studies. In the general population the incidence is 25%-30%.
- Smokers have a high rate of panic attacks.
- Smoking is rare in patients with obsessive-compulsive disorder.

seekers", extroverts change jobs frequently and have a high tolerance for physical pain — an attribute which may come in handy for lifelong smokers. There are degrees of extroversion, and according to Eysenck's study, the more cigarettes you smoke, the more extroverted — and drawn to these stimuluses — you are. On his scale, heavy smokers score 8 for extroversion, occasional puffers 7.1.

Power of negative thinking

Oddly, for people so motivated by the power of chance, smokers have a generally negative outlook on life. Participants in a 1997 survey in Britain and Norway significantly overestimated their chances of developing lung cancer and heart disease. More smokers than non-smokers thought they might be run over or murdered, and believed they had bugger-all chance of winning the lottery.

In short, we seem a dodgy bunch of people. In all the information available about smokers and our ridiculous habit, there is little to suggest that we have any positive personal characteristics. No mention of our boundless wit, natural sociability, self-deprecation or capacity for jollity. Maybe these things can't be measured by science; maybe nobody's interested in researching them.

I did discover, however, something to suggest that we might be more generous than non-smokers. A survey of waiting staff showed that a restaurant's smoking section yielded better tips than its non-smoking tables. Clearly, frittering away £1,500 a year on a slow-motion suicide can damage your stinginess.

'Thanks for the crap genes, folks'

Until recently, I'd never told my parents I smoke. In their eyes, the habit is tantamount to hopping off a cliff or eating broken glass. They'd be less worried if I told them I'd got a job as a knife-thrower's assistant.

So call me naïve, call me chicken, but for 15 years I told myself that there was no point in putting the folks through anguish because, by this time next week, I'd have quit. A major downside to publishing this book is that I've had to come clean, a prospect which filled me with guilt, dread, fear, and more guilt. Until I discovered that I could blame them ...

Apparently, 20 per cent of your susceptibility to smoking is down to your experiences as an individual, 20 per cent is due to your family environment, and a full 60 per cent is genetic. There is no single gene that causes smoking, but many which make it harder for you to quit. Some make nicotine more addictive. Others make you more vulnerable to stress, which in turn can cause you to smoke. Dopamine transporter gene SLC6A3-9 (let's just call it "the jammy git gene") is more common in non-smokers than in smokers. Those blessed with this numerical gem are less likely to start smoking and, if they do start, find it easier to stop.

So in future, when we smokers hurl the insults "I didn't ask to be born" and "You should have thought of that before you hopped into bed together" at our long-suffering parents, we can add "Thanks for the crap genes" to the diatribe. With luck, they'll be too baffled to point out that they had no more choice over their genes than we did.

Some famous smokers who, for one reason or another, are mostly dead

Vaclav Havel Born 1936

Vaclav Havel, president of the Czech Republic, was a heavy smoker for most of his adult life. The former playwright and human rights activist was twice imprisoned in the 1970s and 1980s for his anti-authoritarian views, before being elected president in the wake of the 1989 "Velvet Revolution".

Havel smoked his "last" cigarette in December 1996 with an old pal, the health minister Jan Strasky. Seconds later he entered an operating theatre to have half his cancerous right lung removed. The operation was declared a success — a questionable description for tearing lumps out of somebody's insides, but it achieved its objective. The disease had been caught at an early stage, and Havel made a good recovery, marrying blonde actress Dasha Veskrnova, his junior by twelve years, only eight days after the operation. Although a BBC cameraman caught him smoking on film a few months later, it is believed that he has now quit completely.

Frank Sinatra RIP 1915-1998

"The Voice" wouldn't have been much use if it hadn't been for "The Lungs", and Frank always treated his multi-million-dollar organs with the care they deserved. His professionalism was such that he would stop smoking and drinking a full five days before a major gig and wouldn't start again until, er, the middle of the show, when he often lit a fag and poured himself a glass of Jack Daniels to perform *One For My Baby*. The words would come out of his mouth accompanied by large plumes of smoke.

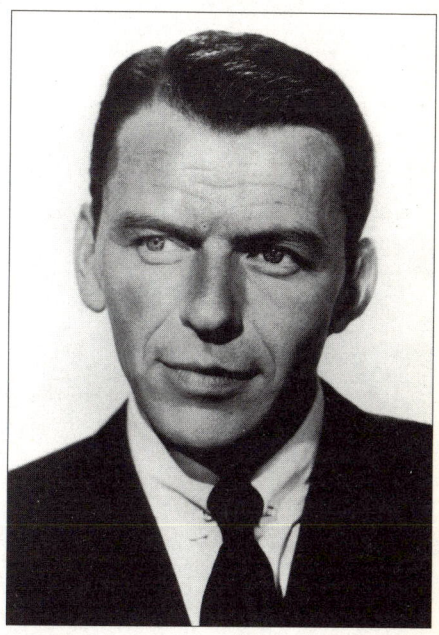

A Camels man when it came to cigarettes, Frank was also partial to a cigar. When the great singer joined the heavenly choir, he had a cigar named after him. Omar Sharif and Alain Delon both achieved this distinction with Asian cigarette brands, but it is unusual for cigars to take their names from entertainers. Manufacturers or sellers (Davidoff, Dunhill etc.) are more common sources. Churchill, Prince Philip and Duke of Wellington are sizes of cigars, not brands. So nice one Frank. And he lived till 82.

3 You-name-it, smoking can seriously damage it

THE SMOKER'S BODY

"I have every sympathy with the American who was so horrified by what he had read of the effects of smoking that he gave up reading." **Henry G. Strauss**

It may surprise you to learn that cigarettes are actually good for you. Smoked in large numbers they reduce a person's chances of getting all kinds of nasty bugs and upsets, and, according to the latest research, their high vitamin content may even help reverse the ageing process. Just kidding. Presumably, during the course of your life to date, you've heard it mentioned that inhaling and exhaling the smoke from cigarettes is, in fact, bad for you. No point beating about the bush on the matter, so here, for the record, we go again.

As a direct result of smoking you may die prematurely of heart disease, stroke, or cancer, particularly of the lung but also the oesophagus, lip, larynx, nose, mouth, bladder, cervix, pancreas or kidneys. Up to one-third of smokers will die from one of these diseases. At the very least, you will probably suffer from impaired

A hardened smoker? You wish

Gents: next time you're enjoying a post-coital cigarette, take a moment to consider that your habit could eventually put an end to the pre-cigarette coitus.

Several reputable scientific studies have shown that smoking impairs a man's ability to achieve an erection. By damaging blood vessels, the smoke inhibits blood flow and reduces the potential maximum of any erection. A "morning glory" is still possible, but it's that bit less glorious than if you didn't smoke. This phenomenon may explain the results of a survey published in the US in 2000, showing that smokers have sex 5.7 times a month, compared with 11.6 times for non-smokers.

In a post-Viagra world the once-taboo subject of impotence has become fair game, and the EU is to advertise this danger on cigarette boxes from 2003. I'm rather looking forward to the campaign: "Smoke till you droop — too many drags and you'll never pull again". All right, I'm being juvenile. But even "Cigarettes shrink your penis" would be superior to the proposed: "Smoking may cause sexual impotence due to decreased blood flow to the penis. This can prevent you from having an erection."

The concept has the potential to shake smokers' belief that cigarettes enhance sex appeal, but not if it's phrased in the sterile officialese of the cigarette pack warning.

circulation, more colds, worse flu, tonsillitis, nosebleeds, and premature skin wrinkling. All these risks are passed on to your children, who through your example are more likely to smoke.

Some doctors refuse to operate on you for illnesses that are the result of your habit — some heavy smokers cannot be given general anaesthetics for certain procedures. You are warned off deep-sea diving and forbidden from space travel, and can probably rule yourself out of running the marathon and (in most cases) for the bus.

The average smoker dies seven years earlier than the average non-smoker. So, in the words of Lloyd Cole, are you ready to be ...

... Heart-broken: One of the main ill-effects of smoking is blood vessel damage or "vasoconstriction". Constricted blood vessels make the heart work harder to deliver oxygen to the body, leading to raised blood pressure. Most seriously, vasoconstriction narrows the arteries, causing coronary heart disease, which kills 26,000 smokers in the UK every year. Cigarettes double your risk of heart attack. As well as hastening death, smoking can cause long-term heart problems such as irregular heartbeat and chronic shortness of breath.

Lung-suffering: Smoking is held responsible for 30% of all cancer deaths, but especially those caused by lung cancer, of which 80% are blamed on smoking. Lung cancer has long been the leading form of the disease in men and has now overtaken breast cancer as the most common form in women. It affects one in four smokers. The risk grows with length of habit and the number of cigarettes smoked.

Lung cancer usually causes death within a year, but other, slightly less common respiratory illnesses cause long-term suffering. Nearly all victims of emphysema and chronic bronchitis — collectively known as chronic obstructive pulmonary disorder — are smokers. In emphysema, air passages in the lungs are enlarged, become inelastic and fail to contract when you breathe out. The condition is irreversible, and many sufferers become dependent on artificial oxygen supply.

Legless: Circulation problems don't just affect the heart. Clotting can block blood supply to the brain, causing stroke, a significant — if not major — cause of death from smoking, especially for women. Elsewhere in the body, "peripheral vascular disease" is characterised by blood clotting in the feet and legs. This causes pain, immobility, then sores on the legs, progressing to gangrene. If it doesn't kill you, it can leave you without a leg to stand on. There are 2,000 amputations every year in the UK as a result.

Shrivelled-up: It's less a blow to health than to vanity, but another consequence of blood vessel damage is the failure to carry blood-borne nutrients to the skin. With the skin's "elastin" damaged, it no longer stretches as it naturally should, and your face ends up looking pretty much as it would in 20 years if you didn't smoke. It's a sort of time-machine effect. Fantastic, eh? As if that wasn't bad enough, the smoke itself dries out your skin, and gets in your eyes, causing

Richter scale for risk

People have funny perceptions of health hazards. We worry that the mobile phone mast half a mile from our house is a death threat, yet will happily drive home from the pub with four pints on board. For those still not convinced that we smokers are slowly doing ourselves in, British statistician Dr Frank Duckworth has developed a "riskometer", running from one to eight, of likelihood of death from certain activities. A 20-a-day habit puts you near the top of the scale — but relax: it isn't quite as dangerous as a session of Russian roulette.

100-mile rail journey	**0.3**
Destructive asteroid impact (in lifetime of a new-born male)	**1.6**
100-mile car journey (sober, middle-aged driver)	**1.7**
Rock-climbing (one session)	**4.2**
Murder (new-born male)	**4.6**
Lifetime car travel (new-born male)	**5.5**
Rock-climbing (over 20 years)	**6.3**
Deep-sea fishing (40-year career)	**6.4**
Smoking (male 35; 20 a day)	**6.9**
Russian roulette (one game)	**7.2**
Suicide	**8.0**

squinting and more wrinkles. On the plus side, there's some evidence that smoking may have a mild protective effect against acne.

And a lot more besides: Smoking aggravates asthma, diabetes and bowel disorders. It weakens your immune system, slows recovery from surgery and illness, and makes you snore. In pregnancy, it can cause a range of problems for both mother and child. And I am shocked to learn that cigarette smoke is also associated with "heavy metal exposure" in children. That may explain the appeal of Marilyn Manson to our younger folk. So, yes, cigarettes really are bad for you.

Time, then, for some good news. Giving up smoking, if you can manage it, will have an immediately positive effect on blood pressure and the heart, and reduce the long-term risk of lung cancer.

In this time	This will happen
20 minutes	Blood pressure and pulse rate return to normal
8 hours	Nicotine and carbon monoxide levels halved
24 hours	Lungs start to clear out mucus
72 hours	Breathing becomes easier. Energy levels increase
2-12 weeks	Circulation improves
3-9 months	Lung function is increased by up to 10%
1 year	Risk of a heart attack falls to half that of a smoker
10 years	Risk of lung cancer falls to half that of a smoker
15 years	Risk of heart attack same as if you'd never smoked

Source: Action on Smoking and Health

The doctors who loved tobacco

Today, it's hard to imagine a time when smoking was considered harmless. In fact, for hundreds of years, Europeans believed it was a healthy pursuit, and the endorsement of tobacco by the medical profession was the principal reason for the plant's acceptance in 16th-century Europe.

Galenic medicine was the dominant philosophy of the time. Galenists believed the human body had four "humours": blood, phlegm, black bile and yellow bile. Each one had an essence. Phlegm was cold and moist; blood was hot and moist. A healthy body balanced the four humours.

The Galenic school also put much faith in discovering a remedy for most, if not all, known diseases. When early travellers to the New World observed that native Americans consumed tobacco in vast quantities and rarely got sick, they thought they had stumbled upon the panacea.

They quickly ascribed all sorts of healing powers to their new discovery. Tobacco — a hot, dry therapy — purged the body of excess fluids. Placed on the skin, its leaves treated cuts and wounds. Chewing it relieved hunger. The wonderdrug even encouraged relaxation.

Any initial scepticism was greatly undermined by a top European physician, the Spaniard Monardes, who in 1571 drew up a list of 20 ailments — from toothache to cancer — which could be cured by tobacco. After this accolade, chewing, snuffing and smoking tobacco took off among health-conscious Europeans, and it took almost 400 years of medical debate for doctors to fully change their minds.

Healthy debates?

It's said that smoking is one of the leading causes of statistics, and the body of information on smoking and health is awash with data (much of it contradictory) that can be utterly bewildering for the poor smoker in the street.

Only recently I heard that stroke risk remains high for up to 20 years after quitting smoking, courtesy of the *Journal of Epidemiology and Community Health.* Hours later, I read in *Cigarettes: What the Warning Label Doesn't Tell You* that stroke risk disappears within two to four years of a person stopping smoking. Whom to believe?

While some of the confusion can be blamed on selective reporting by journalists, much of it is a product of the "tobacco war" between cigarette makers and the health lobby. The tobacco companies want our money, medics want us to have healthy lungs and hearts, and both realise that to win, they must first capture our minds.

Each side carries out scientific research and disseminates it through the media. The tobacco industry used to have the edge in public relations, but as the health lobby has become more organised, medics have proved they are no slouches when it comes to spin-doctoring. During the 1990s, their legal and PR campaign broke the defences of the tobacco industry, which has gone from denying the worst effects of cigarettes to public admission that smoking is carcinogenic, productive of heart disease and respiratory problems, and addictive. A few areas of debate remain, however ...

Controversy 1: Cancer

Since the 1960s, the medical profession — and the public — have accepted that smoking causes lung cancer, but there are people out there who doubt it still. Though it's undeniable that nearly all lung cancer victims are smokers, the way in which smoking affects the lung is not fully understood by scientists. Therefore the relationship is statistical rather than medical, the detractors claim.

In *Smoking, Health and Personality,* the late psychology professor Hans Eysenck points out that lung cancer rates are low in South Africa, Russia and Poland, despite high rates of smoking. He offers the theory that cigarettes smoked in western Europe and the US are more carcinogenic due to their intensive methods of production.

Eysenck has a second theory: that the relationship between smoking and cancer may derive from constitutional features. People with certain physical characteristics (short, squat) and personality types (extroverted) are most vulnerable to cancer, he says. By coincidence, these same people have a tendency towards smoking and other stimulant behaviours. Eysenck argues that the admittedly strong evidence that smoking causes cancer is not conclusive and calls for more open-minded research into other factors.

Controversy 2: Passive smoking

Is passive smoking a health hazard or a political contrivance? It's certainly an important weapon in the armoury of the health lobby. The perceived health threat from second-hand smoke has justified bans on smoking in social areas across the world over the past 15 years. Worries about passive smoking weaken the tobacco industry's economy, leave it open to litigation from non-smokers (bar workers and flight attendants have already sought compensation for alleged smoke-related illnesses), and foster anti-smoking sentiments among non-smokers.

With so much as stake, it's a political contest neither side wants to lose. So anti-smoking scientists insist passive smoking is a major killer, responsible for 3,000 deaths a year in the United States. They cite studies showing that non-smoking wives are more likely to get cancer if their husbands smoke.

The tobacco industry retorts by saying the risk is too small to be statistically significant.

It's clear that the risk of disease from passive smoking is minuscule compared to that from "active" smoking. Passive smoking might cause 3,000 deaths a year in the US, but cancer is said to kill more than 200,000 smokers. Given the relative scale, it will always be easy for the tobacco industry to make passive smoking sound like a non-risk.

Whatever the truth of the matter, the anti-smoking groups' pursuit of this issue is a questionable PR tactic. For consumers of cigarettes — who may die from lung or heart disease, have a limb hacked off, and suffer any of the other unseemly effects outlined above — passive smoking is a triviality. By making an issue of it, the health lobby could be alienating the people it is ultimately trying to help: smokers.

Controversy 3: Diseases of the brain

If there are any health benefits from smoking, they're comfortably outweighed by the habit's many destructive effects on the body. But there is considerable evidence to suggest smokers suffer less from the degenerative diseases, Alzheimer's and Parkinson's.

Smokers have been shown to be 50% less likely than non-smokers to develop Parkinson's disease. Currently, the most popular explanation among medics is that Parkinson's is caused by a deficiency of dopamine in the brain, a deficiency that nicotine helps to correct.

The controversy arises with Alzheimer's, where the research is more complicated. Though early investigations found smoking had a protective effect against the disease, the research which produced these findings has been criticised by the authors of the "Rotterdam" study, which suggested that smoking doubles the risk of Alzheimer's in those with susceptible genes.

Nicotine has also been shown to calm the symptoms of Tourette's syndrome, although if you find yourself being spontaneously abusive to strangers as soon as you quit smoking, it's less likely to be Tourette's syndrome than no-cigarettes syndrome.

Controversy 4: Diet

Another heretic scientist, Dr Ken Denson, of the Thrombosis and Haemostosis Research Foundation in Oxford, shocked the medical world in 1999 when he said that smokers' health problems weren't caused by cigarettes, but by poor diet. The studies demonstrating that smoking causes heart disease and lung cancer had not taken diet into account, he said, and people could get away with smoking fewer than ten a day if only they ate (surprise, surprise) more fruit and veg and less fat.

Denson's pronouncement didn't go down well with the medical establishment, and as someone who begins to feel ropey when I smoke ten cigarettes a day, I can't say I warm to his theory myself.

But it's undeniable that smokers who eat properly have a lower risk of cancer than those with bad diets. We not only deplete essential nutrients through smoking, but also miss out on opportunities to restock them, by smoking when we might otherwise be eating. Smoking inhibits the intake of vitamin C, a deficiency which can be counteracted by taking a 2,000mg supplement each day. In turn, vitamin C aids the absorption of iron, another essential vitamin that smokers often lack.

Since cigarettes contain poisons, the smoker's body needs to stock up on the antioxidants vitamin E, beta carotene, selenium and zinc, which can be achieved by gorging ourselves on fresh fruit and vegetables. It won't stop the rot altogether but eating well can significantly lower your cancer risk.

Which I'm sure cheers you up no end.

Some famous smokers who, for one reason or another, are mostly dead

Sigmund Freud RIP 1865-1945

"Sometimes a cigar is just a cigar," said Freud, but behind Sigmund's light-hearted bon mots lies, as usual, something much darker, deeper, and dirtier. The man was in fact indivertibly addicted to penises — I mean cigars — which he put into his mouth on a regular basis and sucked upon. Hmmm.

The Daddy of Shrinkology puffed his way through 20 cigars a day, yet always remained in a state of denial about what he called his "habit or vice". Instead, he thought cigars enhanced his intellectual powers and self-control. Freud underwent some 30 operations to combat cancer of the soft palate. Even then, the habit gripped him so fiercely that he would force open his mouth with a clothes peg, no matter how painful, to wedge a cigar between his teeth.

Christy Turlington Born 1969

In December 2000, the then 31-year-old supermodel Christy Turlington announced she had emphysema. "When I started modelling I wanted to appear more grown up," she explained. "By 16 I was on a pack a day. The frightening thing is, my smoking caused permanent damage." The former 20-a-day smoker, who gave up in 1995, saw her father die of lung cancer in 1997. Since then she has been an outspoken critic of smoking and has gone from fronting Calvin Klein campaigns to appearing in anti-smoking ads for the NHS in the UK.

Julie Andrews
Born 1935

Poor Julie. Caught in the von Trapp of her wholesome early film roles, she went out of her way to convince the world she could mix it with the bad girls. Later movies saw her strip for the camera, curse like a sailor, and bed her lesbian maid. The curse of Mary Poppins even drove her to became a screen smoker, in *Thoroughly Modern Millie* (1967) and *Star* (1968). I've been unable to confirm reports that she also smoked in real life, but her current state of health leads me to suspect that she might have. Her *Sound of Music* co-star Christopher Plummer was equally haunted by the film that made him famous, and dubbed it "The Sound of Mucus". That, sadly, is a fitting description for Julie's singing voice nowadays. In 1997, she had non-cancerous nodules removed from her throat, leaving her unable to sing again.

4 *Nowhere left to go*
THE SMOKER'S SPACE

Annette: "Sex isn't a relationship."
Helen: "A fag isn't a bus, but I like to have one while I'm waiting."
From: It Was 2pm in the Morning, by Kevin Magee

I became a smoker proper in 1987. If the habit was not exactly encouraged by the establishment then, there were few practical impediments to you spending the whole day with a permanent cloud above your head. On leaving the house in the morning, you'd hop on a bus and head straight for the smoking section upstairs. The only smoker who might contemplate sitting downstairs was one whose circulation was so bad, he'd had his legs lopped off. You could squeeze in two or three cigarettes on the journey to work.

I visited London that year, and noticed that commuters on the Tube were less well catered for, as smoking was prohibited on the trains. But until a tragic fire at King's Cross station led to a ban on smoking in stations that year, you could treat yourself to a cigarette as you waited on the platform. Although lighting up was, of course, a virtual guarantee that your train would come whizzing in to interrupt the moment of pleasure.

And so to work: one big smoking room. With an ashtray on every second desk, a person could quite happily puff their way through five or six fags in the course of a working morning, without ever leaving their desk for a "non-productive" cigarette break.

If you took an afternoon off for an appointment at the hospital (to have, say, a chest X-ray) you could while away the three-hour wait by finishing off the box of ten you bought that morning, then start cadging them from the pregnant woman beside you.

And if, in the evening, you felt like a trip to the cinema, you could comfortably smoke three or four fags an hour while the plot unfolded, then up your quota as the film built to its dramatic finale. Afterwards, a trip to the pub for a heated discussion on the plot and characters provided an opportunity to meet your daily intake of approximately 30 cigarettes.

For this orgy of tobacco consumption, you would pay around £2.50 a day. Although that seemed dear at the time, prices were low enough for you to buy ten cigarettes and a box of matches for under a quid.

Things are different now. "I'd walk a mile for a Camel" ran the copyline of an early tobacco ad. Nowadays, you might have to, such are the restrictions on smoking in public. Waking in the morning, you might just have time for a quick drag as you wait for the bus, snatch a few guilty minutes out of your working day for one-and-a-half smokes, drum your fingers during your four-hour wait in the hospital, bite your nails through a movie, then maybe have to ensure you're sitting in the smoking section when you repair to the pub afterwards.

The £2.50 you spent on 30 cigarettes in 1987 would now buy you a box of 10 and some chewing gum, and to get through any more than that you'd need to structure your day fairly carefully.

Smoking on the edge

The current aim of the anti-smoking movement is to push smoking to the margins of our society, and to make non-smoking the norm. Although governments generate massive tax revenue from cigarette sales, they can no longer deny that smoking is a lethal habit, and accordingly have taken steps to protect the health of their citizens.

Prohibitions on tobacco advertising and sponsorship are either in place or imminent in most European countries. Cigarette prices are not yet at a level that might make smoking an occasional luxury, but they have more than doubled in the past decade, and cheap, duty-free cigarettes can no longer be sold within the EU. Alongside these moves, a broad acceptance of the argument that passive smoking is dangerous has led to controls on smoking in public places.

On the job

Visitors to US cities have been known to express astonishment at the high level of prostitution, even in the main business districts, only to be informed that these are not sex workers but office girls who must take their cigarette breaks out on the street.

In some American firms, smoking is prohibited even when you're not on the job, and your extra-curricular lifestyle can be an important

Accidents waiting to happen

A ban on smoking could make your workplace more dangerous than ever. A couple of years ago I came across a study showing a glut of workplace accidents on National No-Smoking Day.

Apparently, many people who starve themselves of the fumatory poison for the day find themselves so exasperated that they go around dropping girders on their feet, stapling their fingers together, and reversing over colleagues.

As someone who has always blithely ignored No-Smoking Day, the biggest shock was the realisation that many people do actually stop smoking for a day. If you're one of those who see some merit in doing cold turkey for 24 hours in the middle of March, first ask yourself: am I really prepared to put myself and my colleagues in jeopardy?

factor in recruitment. Companies which offer employee health insurance prefer to employ fit non-smokers to keep their medical bills down. In the mid-1990s, an engineering company in Indiana sacked a new employee when it discovered (through a urine test taken during a routine medical) that she had smoked six cigarettes the previous week.

European businesses are a little slower to boot their smokers onto the pavement, either temporarily or permanently, but are increasingly adopting a policy on smoking. That policy is rarely "Smoke as much as you like". In a 1999 British survey, 48% of workers said smoking was not allowed anywhere on the premises where they worked — a leap from 42% who answered the same way two years previously.

Companies introduce no-smoking policies for many reasons. Some are concerned about staff welfare and job-satisfaction levels among non-smokers. Others are paranoid about personal injury claims from staff working in smoky environments. Some just can't stand seeing working hours lost to cigarette breaks.

If you feel persecuted by your company's smoking policy, don't rule out a career change. Many small businesses, pubs and restaurants still allow smoking in the workplace, although not always by staff. If you get a job as a silver-service waiter, you may not be able to swan around with a fag in your mouth, but you could at least catch a whiff if you're assigned to the smoking section (remember: bigger tips).

And why limit yourself to the catering industry: anti-smoking groups estimate that three million workers in Britain are exposed to tobacco smoke, so you should be able to find something to suit you.

Home sweet home

Well, at least we can still smoke at home. Can't we? Well, just about. In 1997, Britain's West, Mid and East Lothian Councils asked people with home-helps not to smoke when their helpers were there. When a home becomes a workplace, the rules change. Faced with a choice, which would you get rid of first: the fags, or the child-minder, cleaner, builder and butler?

Fortunately, that dilemma is beyond the means of most smokers, but even ordinary homes are seeing less fumatory activity. An campaign in the US encourages non-smokers in apartment blocks to complain about smoke from their neighbours' apartments being re-circulated by air-conditioning systems, with the aim of having the buildings declared smoke-free.

And as smokers themselves are swept along in the tide of proscription and health-consciousness, they are curtailing their habits without being asked. Smokers are now less likely to have a cigarette in the presence of people who may not approve — or that's what they tell surveyors at any rate. 60% of British smokers say they wouldn't light up when in a room with a child (up from 54% in 1997) and many say that, in the presence of non-smoking adults, they smoke less or not at all. We could become so obedient that we no longer need to be regulated.

Catering for puffers

In deference to smokers' weakness for an after-dinner cigarette, the catering trade has been left largely to its own devices with regard to smoking restrictions. Some restaurants voluntarily forbid smoking, most have large or small smoking sections, and others lump everyone in together so that smoking and non-smoking tables can battle it out between themselves.

Certain hotels and bed-and-breakfasts have taken advantage of the wave of anti-smoking sentiment and banned smoking in rooms, so that guests don't burn the house down or leave marks on carpets (guilty), furniture (guilty) and the tops of toilet cisterns (well, it's dangerous to wipe your bum with a lit cigarette in your hand).

Pubs: the final frontier

But mercifully, smoking has not yet been outlawed in the local boozer. People who are attracted to one poison are quite likely to indulge in one or two others as well. Apart from recovering alcoholics, who tend to be heavy smokers, there are few smokers who don't drink. Mindful of this, the powerful publicans' lobby has taken care to protect its customers from any legislation that might interfere with their addictions.

Customers may fret if they can't drink and smoke at will, but publicans have to worry about their staff as well as their clientele. In 1999, a group of 50 Irish bar workers announced a series of lawsuits against their employers or former employers, whom they blamed for

Dens of iniquity

Smoking in bars was outlawed in California in 1998, but in the more liberal city of San Francisco, owners were quick to find loopholes. As the ban was primarily designed to protect employees, rather than proprietors, some bars embarked upon shared ownership schemes.

Terraces were not covered by the ban, so other establishments extended their smoking area into a car park. Also, customers could smoke in areas not served by waiting staff, so a self-service culture quickly developed. And since the police penalised just five establishments in the law's first year of operation, many bars just ignored it altogether.

their smoking-related illnesses.

The cases suggest there is one word that might make the publicans think again: compo. Shortly afterwards, a scheme to improve ventilation in Irish pubs was introduced, and there were moves at government level to open designated smoking areas in bars. For now, these probably represent the short-term future of smoking in pubs.

But don't expect things to change too fast. The British catering industry has a charter with the government to voluntarily improve air quality and to create smoking and non-smoking sections. Although the 2001 *Good Pub Guide* claims two-thirds of public houses now have no-smoking sections, a survey in March 2000 showed only 1% of establishments had complied with the government charter.

The curious case of the disappearing cigarettes

It is conceivable that, in a couple of generations, not only will there be no smokers left on the planet, but no evidence of anybody ever having smoked. Sounds daft? Some people would have it so.

Take novelist Alexandra Campbell. Worried that product placement in movies was causing an increase in "fictional smoking", she resolved in January 2001 to create no more smoking characters in her books. "If Chaucer, Shakespeare and Jane Austen could portray fully rounded characters without making them smokers, then so can I," she declared. Campbell's decision to set her stories in a non-smoking world might cause her work to be recategorised as science fiction, but at least she's not trying to rewrite history. Others are quite prepared to take that step.

In 1997 members of Pembrokeshire County Council sought to rehabilitate Isambard Kingdom Brunel, the great engineer of the Industrial Revolution, as a non-smoker. A likeness of Brunel was to appear on road signs in the town of Neyland, Wales, where his steamships once docked. But council members were concerned that the best-known picture of Brunel showed him smoking a cigar and suggested that the offending article be removed in the artwork, lest they be seen to endorse smoking.

Three years previously, the governors of the Isambard Brunel School at Portsmouth had successfully airbrushed out the cigar for similar reasons. This time, sanity mercifully prevailed, and old Isambard Kingdom was allowed to puff away to his heart's content (or discontent as the case may be). It might have occurred to the anti-smokers that Brunel would be more use to them with a cigar than without, given that he died at the relatively early age of 53.

What next? Sherlock Holmes without a pipe? *The Thunderbirds'* Lady Penelope Creighton-Ward without her trademark cigarette holder? Could be.

In 2001, the Roy Castle Lung Cancer Foundation made representations to the BBC to alter scenes from *Thunderbirds* in which Lady Penelope and Parker, her butler, smoke cigarettes, on the basis that the programme was watched by children. "Seeing so many characters with a cigarette or cigar will give a young audience the impression that smoking is cool or to be admired," the charity argued. "With modern technology it must be possible to alter these scenes to take away the cigarette." The BBC refused, saying that the puppet show was not specifically aimed at children.

Elsewhere in the media, legal advisers caution publishers about printing pictures of people smoking, lest they be construed as publicity for the habit.

The idea of all this censorship is to stamp out positive images of a dangerous habit, but denying the existence of a social problem is no way to eradicate it. The fact is, smoking is still practised by more than one-quarter of our population. Though I don't want to see it falsely promoted as a positive or health-giving act, to edit it out of books, photographs, newspapers and TV as though it no longer occurs — or never did — is a distortion of the truth.

Some famous smokers who, for one reason or another, are mostly dead

William Jefferson Clinton
Born 1946

The public don't know for sure if Bill Clinton is a secret smoker. Though for eight years he was pulled up on nearly every false move — draft dodging, tax dodging, monogamy dodging — nobody really went after him for smoking.

He entered the White House in January, 1993, amid claims that he had toasted his electoral success with a cigar, and just after the campaign in which he had been accused of smoking hash in Oxford. During his two terms, cameras often caught the president with an unlit cigar in his mouth, but never actually smoking.

For his part, Bill denied that he smoked, insisted he was allergic to cigars, and pointed out that a smoking president would have been a bad example to the public. I personally stopped caring whether or not he lit his cigars after the Starr report revealed his far more creative uses for the old stogies when in the company of Ms Monica Lewinksy.

John F Kennedy RIP
1917-1963

In the battle of the presidents, John F Kennedy seems miles ahead of Bill Clinton. For starters, he cheated with Marilyn Monroe where Bill chose Monica Lewinsky, and smoked Cuban cigars where Clinton um, employed, Dominicans. In a morality contest it's *nul points* all round. But when it comes to patriotism, Bill might just shade it over JFK. While Clinton considered it high treason to smoke Cuban cigars, Kennedy had no such qualms.

In 1960, just before cutting off trade between the US and Cuba, Kennedy dispatched two aides to scour the tobacconists of Washington and buy up as many Havanas as they could lay hands on. They returned with over 1,000 cigars. Later that year, in a conciliatory gesture, Che Guevara asked a White House envoy to take a box of cigars back to Kennedy in the US. The president took the cigars, but broke off diplomatic relations shortly afterwards.

Kennedy, like a lot of sinners, probably saw no hypocrisy in his actions and may have reasoned, like many cigar-loving US patriots, that in smoking Cuban cigars he was not supporting a socialist economy, "just burning their fields".

5 Who is 'Big Tobacco'?

THE TOBACCO INDUSTRY

"Some women would prefer having smaller babies."
Joseph Cullman, Philip Morris President, 1971

Americans just love putting the word "big" in front of things, hence this sobriquet for the cigarette industry. Just four companies dominate the world tobacco trade. Three of these originated in the United States or Britain but are now multinationals whose cigarettes are smoked all over the world. The fourth is the Chinese National

Tobacco Company, which is the world's biggest producer of cigarettes, but nearly all for use within Chinese borders.

As "mature" markets, Britain and Ireland have little exposure to these multinationals. 80% of the cigarettes smoked here are made by Gallaher and Imperial Tobacco, which have been based in these islands for over 100 years, though both now have significant international interests.

The big three
Philip Morris
Major brands: Marlboro, Virginia Slims, Chesterfield, Philip Morris

Profile: Founded as a tobacconists' shop on Bond Street, London in the mid-19th century, Philip Morris moved to the US in 1902 and is now the world's largest tobacco multinational, largely due to the success of its flagship brand, Marlboro, the world number one. PM has significant interests in every region of the world and controls more than half the market in the US, where stockbrokers call it "Big Mo".

Dirty tricks: The "Whitecoat Project" appointed scientific consultants to the tobacco company to influence scientific and public opinion. These consultants were used to orchestrate controversy around passive smoking and other smoking issues, and to act as witnesses in litigation. PM lawyers successfully infiltrated the medical journal, the *Lancet,* by appointing one of its editors as a consultant.

Any other business? Owns food multinational Kraft — whose products include Maxwell House, Philadelphia and Dairylea — and Miller Beer.

British American Tobacco

Major brands: Carrolls, Rothmans, Lucky Strike

Profile: BAT, the second-biggest tobacco multinational in the world, was founded in the early 1900s as part of a corporate truce between US and British tobacco firms. Today it describes itself as the world's "most international" tobacco company, with interests in every continent. Among others, it owns Carrolls in Ireland, Rothmans in the UK, and Brown & Williamson and American Brands in the US. Former British chancellor Ken Clarke is a board member.

Dirty tricks: BAT failed to pursue development of less carcinogenic cigarettes on the basis that marketing them as "safe" could leave them vulnerable to litigation. "In attempting to develop a 'safe' cigarette you are, by implication, in danger of being interpreted as accepting that the current product is 'unsafe' and this is not a position that I think we should take," said the BAT chairman in 1986.

Any other business? Formerly owned the insurance companies Eagle Star and Allied Dunbar and the discount shop Argos, but sold them in 1997 to concentrate on tobacco.

RJ Reynolds/Japan Tobacco International

Major brands: Camel, More, Winston, Salem

Profile: RJ Reynolds began life as an all-American company, naming its brands after its home town (Winston-Salem, North Carolina) and building its biggest factory in the nearby Tobaccoville. A pioneering company, in 1913 it developed the first mass-market cigarette,

Camel, which remained America's most popular brand for decades. RJR was the first to sell cigarettes in packs of 20 and 10, and in the 1950s made the first commercially successful filtered cigarette, Winston. It has also test-marketed the "safer" cigarettes Premier and Eclipse. In 1999, RJR sold its international business to Japan's national tobacco company to create Japan Tobacco International, the world's third-largest tobacco company.

Dirty tricks: Smuggling. The European Commission has accused RJR and Philip Morris of participating in a worldwide cigarette-smuggling scheme. According to court papers, the two companies "control, direct, encourage, support, promote and facilitate the smuggling of cigarettes into the European Community".

Britain & Ireland
Gallaher
Brands: Benson & Hedges, Silk Cut, Hamlet cigars
Profile: Gallaher, which has its origins in Northern Ireland, is the biggest tobacco company in the UK, the Republic of Ireland and Russia. In the British and Irish markets, it is a major sponsor of sports, including rugby league (Silk Cut), golf, snooker, and Eddie Jordan's Formula 1 team (all Benson & Hedges).
Dirty tricks: Knew of but denied the lung cancer link for 30 years. In 1970, the General Manager of Research at Gallaher wrote a memo saying: "We are of the opinion that the Auerbach's work proves beyond reasonable doubt the causation of lung cancer by smoke."

When this document became public in 1998, the company said it had considered the research at the time but rejected the conclusions.

Imperial Tobacco
Brands: John Player, Lambert & Butler, Embassy, St Bruno (for pipes)
Profile: Under threat of competition from America, 13 British tobacco firms merged in 1901 to create the Imperial Tobacco Company. Now, it is a major player in Britain and Ireland, and a significant force in foreign markets. Its John Player Blue brand is the top seller in Ireland. Imperial sponsors the Embassy Snooker Championships.
Any other business: Owns Rizla, Europe's leading brand of cigarette papers, which (my lawyers tell me I should point out) have nothing whatsoever to do with cannabis.

State companies

Britain, Ireland and the United States are unusual in not having national tobacco companies, which are such nice little earners for economies large and small all over the world. They're also the reason you're confronted by so many unheard-of brands while on holiday abroad.

Most state companies produce only for their domestic markets but some, such as Japan, are major international players. Germany's Reemstma has interests in eastern Europe, and Altadis — a merger of the French and Spanish state bodies — produces the well-known French brands Gauloises and Gitanes.

6 A land called Sue

COURTROOM DRAMA

"Sue the bastards."
Motto of John Banzhaf, founder of Action on Smoking and Health

America's relationship with smoking is unlike that of any other country. On the one hand, it introduced tobacco to the world, built its early economy around this cash crop, and benefits still from the industry's massive profits. The infrastructure, economy and culture of the south-eastern states are built around tobacco.

Yet the same country is home to the most successful anti-smoking movement in the world. With a convert's zeal, this lobby has waged a decades-long war on tobacco and its derivative products, securing smoking bans in almost all public places, severely restricting advertising, and procuring billions of tobacco-industry dollars to fund anti-smoking campaigns.

But a politically successful lobby can easily become estranged from its own grassroots. I have always resented those who ticked me off for being foolish enough to indulge in a practice that damages my health, public campaigns which told me I was throwing away money or ruining my features, and doctors who refused to operate on smokers

Types of litigation

There are three main types of cases against the tobacco industry in America.

Individual actions, taken by sick smokers or, if they have died, their families. There are almost 2,000 individual cases pending against the industry in the US.

Class actions, in which a large number of people sue a tobacco firm for collective injuries.

Government actions. Individual states also sued the tobacco industry in the 1990s, to recoup the costs of medical bills for sick smokers. Many of these cases were dropped as part of a mass-settlement in 1998.

with heart disease because they had caused their own illness. Well-intentioned efforts to make me hate cigarettes were wasted.

The people who changed my mind were America's lawyers. In a few short years, the US legal profession — with its usual high-minded goal of making its members even richer than they already are — achieved what decades of anti-smoking publicity failed to do: they made me feel wronged.

In the early 1990s, some of the US's toughest and most successful litigators sat down and planned a new strategy against the tobacco industry. Previous efforts to take on cigarette manufacturers in the courts had been defeated by teams of crack defence lawyers — retained at great expense by the tobacco firms, who had never paid a cent to compensate a sick smoker. But this group knew that if they stuck together to prove that tobacco companies had knowingly sold cancer-causing products, then the industry could be held liable for thousands of illnesses and deaths, and forced to pay compensation.

What emerged in the ensuing court cases across the US set the public reeling. The accusers showed the courts thousands of internal tobacco industry documents, building up a picture of a cynical, paranoid industry which would resort to any low strategy if it meant more smokers and more profits.

What the courts discovered

Throughout the 20th century, tobacco companies told the public that smoking was not addictive and that it hadn't been proven to damage health. In private, they were saying just the opposite.

Cancer confirmed: Numerous documents show that the tobacco industry became aware of the link between smoking and cancer around the same time as the medical establishment did.
And I quote: "Studies of clinical data tend to confirm the relationship between heavy and prolonged tobacco smoking and incidence of cancer of the lung." *Survey of cancer research for RJ Reynolds, 1953.*

Spin was king: When this was discovered, many scientists working for the tobacco industry favoured eradicating the more dangerous compounds in cigarettes. But the industry's approach was dictated by its lawyers and PR consultants. Their strategy was to sow doubt in the minds of the public over whether or not smoking was truly dangerous.
And I quote: "The most important type of story is that which casts

doubt in the cause and effect theory of disease and smoking. Eye-grabbing headlines were needed and should strongly call out the point — Controversy! Contradiction! Other Factors! Unknowns!"
Article by PR consultant in Tobacco and Health Research, 1968.

Addiction accepted: The word addiction was used within the industry as early as the 1950s, and it was quickly established that allure of cigarettes lay in the addictive drug nicotine.
And I quote: "Smoking is an addictive habit attributable to nicotine, and the form of nicotine affects the rate of absorption by the smoker."
From a BAT scientists' conference, 1967.
And I quote some more: "It has been suggested that cigarette smoking is the most addictive drug. Certainly large numbers of people will continue to smoke because they can't give it up. If they could they would do so. They can no longer be said to make an adult choice."
Transcript note by a doctor working for BAT, 1980.

Then hushed up: The tobacco companies knew not only that their product damaged health, but also that people couldn't help consuming it. They also knew that if they didn't suppress this information, it could form the basis for lawsuits against the industry.
And I quote: "The entire matter of addiction is the most potent weapon a prosecuting attorney can have in a lung cancer/cigarette case. We can't defend continued smoking as 'free choice' if the person was 'addicted'." *Tobacco Institute document, 1980.*

The big payouts

Juries have ordered several huge awards in US courts. But the fines that make the headlines are usually significantly reduced on appeal.

2001, California: Richard Boeken, a cancer victim who had overcome addictions to alcohol and heroin but couldn't quit smoking, was awarded $5.5 million, and Philip Morris was ordered to pay $3 billion in punitive damages. Reduced to $100 million on appeal.

2000, California: A woman who has since died of lung cancer was awarded $22 million. Under appeal.

1999, California: Philip Morris ordered to pay punitive damages of $50 million, plus $1.5 million compensation to the former smoker and lung cancer victim who had taken the case. The damages were cut to $25 million on appeal.

1999, Florida: Industry ordered to pay $145 billion (yes that's a B) in a class action by a union health care plan. Ongoing appeals.

1999, Oregon: $81 million for the family of deceased smoker Jesse Williams, cut to $32 million on appeal.

The safe smoke supressed: Companies failed to pursue development of less carcinogenic cigarettes on the basis that marketing them as "safe" could leave them vulnerable to litigation. Instead they chose to manufacture low-tar cigarettes, even though they knew these offered no health benefits due to the way they are smoked. **And I quote:** "Marlboro Lights cigarettes were not smoked like regular Marlboros. In effect, the ... smokers in this study did not achieve any reduction in smoke intake by smoking [Marlboro Lights]." *From a 1975 Philip Morris memo.*

And there's more

Around the world, the industry has been implicated in the illegal activities of tobacco smuggling and price-fixing. It has been proven that cigarette advertising deliberately targeted underage smokers. The industry has furthermore been shown to have manipulated the truth about smoking by buying off prominent scientists working in cancer research and medical publishing, and by placing articles in newspapers and magazines that poured cold water on the received wisdom about health risks.

The media reported these cases faithfully, and the cigarette companies became mired in negative publicity. Even John Grisham cashed in with a novel on the subject.

For smokers, the revelations blew a hole in the idea that we were engaged in any act of rebelliousness or expression of personal freedom. Clearly, we had all this time been doing the bidding of powerful corporations, who had robbed us of our money and our health, while lining their already deep pockets.

Smokers, it appears, dislike being the dupes of corporations. A survey in the US found people were more likely to give up smoking

Cases closer to home

Following the US experience, lawsuits against the tobacco industry are in progress all over the world. In Ireland, some 300 people are suing the industry, 200 of them part of a class action.

The biggest case to date in the UK, a group action involving 50 smokers with lung cancer, failed in 1999 because the majority of the claimants had not brought their case within three years of being diagnosed with the disease. Apart from that case, several people have successfully sued their employers over passive smoking.

Ireland's Department of Health and Britain's NHS have both taken advice on suing the tobacco industry to recoup the costs of treating smoking-related diseases, but to date neither has done anything about it.

after learning of the actions of cigarette manufacturers than as a result of health-based anti-smoking information.

The law is an ash

It's undoubtedly true that the tobacco industry has been singled out so that lawyers could make a killing. Scratch the surface of any business — food, brewing, pharmaceuticals, arms — and you'll find evidence of double standards, dodgy science and disregard for human suffering.

It's also true that the central purpose of these cases has not been to win compensation for ill smokers or their relatives. The ongoing litigation also has the political aim of weakening the tobacco industry by imposing huge punitive damages.

The cases are an ingenious PR exercise by the anti-smoking movement. Only through the courts could all those commercially sensitive memos and documents have reached the public.

Many of the cases were dropped in 1998, when the industry agreed to a nationwide out-of-court settlement. In return, the companies agreed to severely limit advertising and promotion, to disband the scientific bodies it had set up, and to pay $206 billion over 25 years towards health research, anti-smoking campaigns, and the treatment of smoking-related diseases.

And tobacco companies now freely admit many of the things they denied for 50 years.

On **www.philipmorris.com**, you can now find the following text: "We agree with the overwhelming medical and scientific consensus that cigarette smoking causes lung cancer, heart disease, emphysema and other serious diseases in smokers. Smokers are far more likely to develop serious diseases, like lung cancer, than non-smokers ... We agree with the overwhelming medical and scientific consensus that cigarette smoking is addictive."

As the PR kings try to spin Big Tobacco out of this ignominy, honesty appears to be the new policy.

Sue a tobacco firm and make your fortune

If a lifetime of smoking has left you with paper-thin lungs, then you might be tempted to wheedle some cash out of the people who fed you cigarettes all those years.

But suing the tobacco industry takes more than just lungs of paper — you'll also need nerves of steel. Cigarette companies staunchly defend all cases against them, often resorting to delaying tactics to bleed the plaintiff of funds until they are forced to drop the case. As RJ Reynolds described its 40-year winning streak in the US: "The way we won these cases, to paraphrase General Patton, is not by spending all of Reynolds' money, but by making the other son of a bitch spend all of his."

Even if you make it to the end, there may be no big payout. Cases in Britain and Ireland are heard by judges, not juries, and those old codgers are far less likely than 12 angry Americans to make big awards.

In the only major case in the UK to date, the solicitor sought £50,000 for each of his 50 clients — better then a poke in the eye with a burning cigar, but a mere drop in the ashtray compared to some of the generous sums awarded across the Atlantic. And the case failed.

Some famous smokers who, for one reason or another, are mostly dead

Humphrey Bogart RIP 1899-1957

Scientists at the University of California have proved it's easier to quit smoking if you live a non-smoking household. Small wonder then that Humphrey Bogart — watching one of the all-time-great advertisements for the habit, Lauren Bacall, puffing away like a train — smoked till the day he died.

Bogart, a heavy smoker and drinker, and a founder of the Hollywood "Rat Pack" of the 1950s, became the quintessential screen smoker after films like *To Have and Have Not*, *The Big Sleep*, and of course *Casablanca*. He was diagnosed with cancer of the oesophagus in early 1956 and, following surgery, became bed-ridden late that year.

But even when he was too weak to walk, he would dress every day in a smoking jacket, go downstairs in a dumb waiter, and — with drink and cigarette in hand — play host to old friends. He died in a coma one Monday morning, aged 57.

Alex Higgins Born 1949

Alex Higgins started smoking before he became a professional snooker player, but only after he became involved in a sport that was inextricably linked with its tobacco sponsors was he offered free cigarettes.

Higgins turned pro in 1971, just a few years after tobacco ads had been banned from television. With cigarette companies looking for alternative exposure on TV, sports sponsorship was an obvious route. "Cigarettes were everywhere but strewn on the floor — every table, every bar," Higgins recalls. "If you're around the product you've got to smoke it eventually, especially when there's booze on the premises. And there was always booze available."

Higgins gave up cigarettes in 1996. Now recovering, hopefully, from throat cancer and having had "a gland or something removed", he calls the people who worked for tobacco companies in his playing days "an insincere shower of bastards". In 1999 he announced he would sue the companies which produce Benson & Hedges and Embassy cigarettes.

"I would say to any young man or woman, leave the dreaded tobacco out of your life. I disagree with the product. I think it's filthy. I'm these days totally against smoking. In the end it'll get you. It'll shorten your life. I was naïve."

7 *The world is your smoking room*

THE SMOKER'S PLANET

"Politicians have felt that smokers are a constituency to whom you can do just about anything and get away with it."
Bill Neville, President, Canadian Tobacco Manufacturers' Council

Ever get the feeling you're not wanted? Do you seethe with anger when told you can't have an after-dinner cigarette because you're sitting at the wrong end of a restaurant? Does your gut contract every time you hand over four pounds for a box of fags? Does your memory stray to a bright summer's day 20 years ago, when you sat in a darkened cinema and happily puffed your way through 30 John Player Special and nobody faked a coughing fit?

Or do you find this society all too permissive? Maybe you're one of those masochist smokers who prefers to be snapped at for lighting up in the house of a friend, because prohibitions are the only thing that stop you devouring two packs a day. You could be a health freak trapped in the body of a self-destructive cigarette junkie, just waiting for the right environment to set you free.

Whatever your feelings, somewhere in the world, no matter which point of the compass you follow, there's a place that will accommodate the peculiarities of your personal habit.

North

Situated, as we are, deep in the northern hemisphere, the possibilities are limited, but there are several places further north where the tobacco culture is quite different to the one you're accustomed to.

If you're partial to the veggie-eating, exercise-bike-riding, wrap-me-in-seaweed sort of vacation, then why not book in for a spot of "nico-tourism" in **Scotland.** Roundelwood Health Spa in Crieff outside Edinburgh (00-44-1764-653806) offers quit-smoking holidays among its special-interest breaks, which also include golfing holidays, retreats for women, and flower arranging courses. Flower arranging? Well it'll give you something to do with your hands.

While **Danes** and **Norwegians** are still avid smokers, **Finland** and **Sweden** are the world's smoking backwaters, with the lowest consumption of cigarettes in the EU. If you're sickened by smoking but still want a non-clinical nicotine hit, hit Sweden, whose inhabitants

The world can't smoke enough

As we witness the crusade against tobacco in the US, and see fewer people smoking in public closer to home, it would be easy to conclude that the world's cigarette makers are ready to wave the white flag. In fact their global position is stronger than ever.

As the international firms enter more new markets, worldwide cigarette consumption is rising. In 1982, the world smoked 4,500 billion cigarettes, and multinationals could sell to only 40% of the world market. Ten years later the multinationals had access to 95% of the world market, and had boosted global consumption to 5,400 billion cigarettes worldwide.

Since the 1960s, smoking in the Western world has been decreasing, to a point where 200 million men and 100 million women smoke. This makes it a far less significant market for cigarettes than developing countries, where 700 million men and 100 million women smoke. The low proportion of smoking women in these societies means the habit has huge growth potential.

What does this trend mean for smokers in this part of the world? Well, profits made abroad give the companies cash and political clout at home. As long as the multinationals remain politically strong in their own back yards, they can make it more difficult for Western governments to restrict smoking and tobacco advertising. In short, it gives us a stay of execution — so to speak.

consume vast quantities of a moist oral snuff. Snuff regained popularity there in the 1960s, when a government anti-smoking campaign pushed it as a healthy alternative to cigarettes, and is now consumed by an estimated 800,000 people.

Medical opinion is divided on the health implications. One study has estimated that oral snuff use caused more cases of cancer in Sweden than the 1986 Chernobyl disaster, and also linked it to heart trouble. Another found that snuff users are 128 times less likely than smokers to develop tumours. Before joining the EU, Sweden had to be exempted from a pan-community ban on "moist snuff", the non-powdered variety favoured by its citizens. Though powdered snuff is still available in your local tobacconist, Sweden is now the only EU country where you can legally buy the softer stuff.

South

Where to begin? The southern hemisphere is the smoking room of the world. Smoking is widespread in countries where the Muslim faith holds sway, even though defilement of the body breaches Islamic law and alcohol remains anathema to most Muslims. Cigarettes appear to have won popular immunity from the sharia, but its teachers do occasionally invoke it to drive home an anti-smoking message.

A campaign in **Bangladesh** in the 1990s used the Koran to discourage smoking. A leaflet sent to the country's religious teachers pointed out that smoking defies the Koran on several counts. Among other things, it is poisonous, suicidal, homicidal (on account of passive smoking), addictive, and an environmental nuisance. Around the same time, in **Egypt,** a Muslim leader issued a fatwa — which means a religious decree, not a death sentence — forbidding smoking. Still, 45% of Egyptian men smoke, even though the country is predominantly Sunni Muslim.

World Bank figures indicate that Muslim men smoke a lot but women barely at all. This is true of **Iraq** (40% of males, 5% of females), **Lebanon** (53% of males, negligible number of females), **Uzbekistan** (40% of males, 1% of females), **Malaysia** (49% of males, 4% of females), **Pakistan** (36% of males, 4% of females), **Saudi Arabia** (40% of males, 8% of females) and **Sudan** (24% of males, 2% of females). An exception to this trend is **Turkey** (51% of males, 49% of females).

In Asia, the most significant market is **China.** To say that the people of China smoke a lot is like saying that Mao Zedong is slightly more left-wing than Tony Blair. You know the statistic about every cigarette taking five minutes off your life? Well, the Chinese smoke so much that they should be into minus figures by now. And the number of smokers (currently 350 million, about as many as in the EU, the US and eastern Europe combined) is increasing by 10% a year.

If you're the kind of smoker who grumbles a lot about living in a health-fascist, anti-smoking nanny state, try moving to China. Granted, the place has its drawbacks: no voting, no private property, plus the presence of a fledgling anti-smoking lobby. This one country smokes one-third of all tobacco worldwide, and its state factories constitute the world's biggest tobacco company. If you can't do much else there, you can smoke like hell.

Needless to say, multinationals hate to see all that money stay in China when they could have a slice of it for themselves, and they have taught the Chinese a thing or two about kow-towing in their efforts to secure a position in this golden-goose market. The Western companies hope that increasing their sales in China and elsewhere in Asia will compensate for declining smoking rates at home. China has been among the toughest Asian markets to crack, and only recently has given restricted access to multinationals.

They have fared better elsewhere in Asia, especially **Japan** and **Taiwan**, where they now hold one-fifth of a growing market. In the midst of Japan's economic crisis in the mid-1990s, the country's chain-smoking prime minister Ryutaro Hashimoto said he would continue smoking "as much as possible", as taxes on smoking were a big source of revenue. The prime minister was not just being patriotic (the Japanese government owns 66% of Japan Tobacco and is obliged by law to promote the sale of cigarettes) but was also possibly hoping his comments would appeal to voters. More than half of Japanese men smoke, compared with less than a third in most Western nations.

In **India** and **Bangladesh**, global conglomerates are weaning locals off the traditional hand-rolled "bidis" in favour of manufactured cigarettes. Only 20% of smokers in India smoke cigarettes as we know them. So BAT has bought one-third of the national tobacco company and has set about creating a cheap alternative to the bidi roll-ups: a revolutionary miniature cigarette.

But travel further south again, to **Australia** and **New Zealand**, and you will encounter some of the world's most fervent anti-smoking movements. Cigarette boxes in Australia are dominated by enormous health warnings. These two countries have some of the lowest smoking rates in the world, at around one quarter of their populations.

East

Europeans are by no means the world's most enthusiastic smokers, but many countries on the mainland are far more tolerant of the practice than Britain or Ireland. Despite moves at EU level against tobacco production and consumption, nearly every state in Europe has an ambivalent attitude to smoking, because they all make such huge direct profits from it.

While Britain, Ireland and the US raise money through taxes on tobacco products, others — including **France, Spain** (whose companies have now merged), **Germany, Denmark, Italy** and **Greece**

Europe's heaviest smokers

	% Female	% Male	All
Greece	28	46	37
Netherlands	33	39	36
Austria	27	42	35
Spain	25	42	33
Denmark	33	37	33
France	23	36	30
Ireland	29	28	29
Luxembourg	26	32	29
UK	28	29	28
Belgium	22	31	26
Germany	20	33	26
Italy	17	33	25
Finland	18	27	22
Sweden	22	17	20
Portugal	7	30	18

Source: World Health Organisation, 1990s

— also have state tobacco companies, which are further sources of revenue to their governments. Probably not coincidentally, those countries which manufacture their own cigarettes tend to have higher rates of smoking than those without.

The fall of Communism in eastern Europe — now one-tenth of the world market — has been a major catalyst to the growth of smoking around the world. In the early 1990s, while most Western entrepreneurs were wondering how to tackle the obstacles of poor banking and unreliable telecommunications in the post-Communist countries, tobacco multinationals lost no time.

When East Germany first opened its borders to Western business, the newly arrived officials from British American Tobacco (BAT) took immediate advantage of the undeveloped economy. Its officials moved into caravans and used taxis to send messages, and by 1992 its HB and Pall Mall brands led the higher priced sector there. BAT is now the leading multinational in unified Germany, and also controls around 50% of the Hungarian market.

Philip Morris, maker of Marlboros, had already been selling cigarettes to **Russia**. In four years under the new rules it bought into three companies in Russia, snapped up a factory in the former **East Germany**, and established a joint venture with the **Czech Republic** monopoly, Tabak. RJ Reynolds targeted **Kazakhstan** and got a foothold in **East Germany**, as did late-arrival Rothmans International. Every market has welcomed at least one multinational.

The former Eastern Bloc countries are less concerned with health than with secure jobs, industrial progress and community development. Tobacco consumption is high — 1,500 cigarettes per person per year in Russia, **Romania** and the Czech Republic; 2,500 per person in **Hungary** and **Poland** — and rising. There are fewer advertising restrictions, and locals like the exotic Western brands.

Though profits are still slow due to sluggish economic expansion, the tobacco firms have modernised and reorganised the industry in that part of the world. They can afford to wait for their investments to mature, even if sales continue to dwindle at home.

West

An Tobair, a pub in Galway city on the west coast of **Ireland**, became Ireland's first non-smoking pub in April 1999. But before you go rushing off in search of this Spartan drinking den, you should know that it lifted the ban six weeks later after it lost most of its customers. So it's much like any other pub you're familiar with.

Beyond Galway, the possibilities are limited, as it's mostly ocean. Even counting the possibility that the lost city of **Atlantis** still exists, it's doubtful its inhabitants have very developed smoking habits.

You could go farther, and pay a visit to Uncle Sam and Anti-Smoking. Unless you are actually a recent arrival from the lost city of Atlantis — and haven't already read the previous chapters — you probably know that as a whole the **United States** is inhospitable to keen smokers, but offers interesting financial opportunities to addicts suffering from terminal lung cancer who don't mind spending, say, the next decade sitting in a courtroom.

And, in the most politically correct land in the world, you have to watch not just where you light up, but how you talk. Remember, this is the country where "I'm going out to smoke a fag" might be taken to mean you're going to kill a homosexual.

However, the US is also one of the world's largest growers of tobacco and producers of cigarettes. It is home to a great diversity of attitudes and cultures, some of which are quite well-disposed to "terbaccy" and its products. Its federal political system ensures that laws, institutions and even cigarette prices can vary from state to state. For example, Georgia and Kentucky in the south-east have a far more liberal attitude to smoking than west-coast states such as California, probably the most avidly anti-smoking region in the world, where it is forbidden to smoke inside bars or within 20 feet of a public building. A rough rule of thumb is that the further north you go, the less receptive they are to smoking in general.

Which brings us to **Canada,** where only about one-quarter of the population still smoke. An intensive anti-smoking campaign has secured tough restrictions on smoking in public places and workplaces (smoking rooms are forbidden if even one employee objects), an outright ban on tobacco advertising, a prohibition on smoking in bars in Toronto, and health warnings in text and graphics covering half the front surface of cigarette packets, which incidentally are among the most expensive in the world.

It seems ironic that north America, the original home of tobacco and a colony founded on the economy of the "golden leaf", should now be the world's least enthusiastic consumer of the stuff. And, as the destination for most of the profits from cigarette consumption worldwide, the US seems more than willing to count the cash as the rest of the world counts the invalids. You can smoke all you want, Uncle Sam seems to say, but not in my backyard.

Mile-high misery

Travel may broaden the mind, but it doesn't do much for a smoker's nerves. To get anywhere worth going to, we have to sit in a high-altitude torture chamber breathing tinned air for hours on end, usually completely without cigarettes. Bearing in mind that just sitting in an aeroplane can make you ill — the recycled air predisposes flyers to colds, flu, and throat and eye infections — it's a bit rich that most airlines now forbid smoking.

The bans are not so much to benefit passengers, but to protect in-flight staff and, ultimately, the flight companies themselves. In 1991 in the United States, a lawsuit was taken by a group of non-smoking air stewards who had contracted smoking-related diseases. Although the action was against tobacco companies (who eventually settled for $300 million), airlines could also be open to such litigation. If outside regulation doesn't put an end to all smoking in aircraft, the threat of court action eventually will.

For those of us trying to kick the habit, flying is the easy part of the trip. After touching down at the other end, the theoretically pleasant holiday becomes a horror of pitfalls and temptations. Born-again puritans who have been clean for months quickly revert to type while boozing in the sunshine with their brand-new best pals. Weak-willed idealists who left home with high hopes and noble intentions touch down at the other end with lowered expectations and an armoury of self-deceiving excuses.

You give me air rage

A worrying number of air rage incidents seem to be linked to smoking — or its enforced absence. And it's not just smokers who suffer. Those who get frustrated on non-smoking flights might take some comfort from the case of John Bagwell, an anti-smoker who got his comeuppance on a flight to London from South Africa in December

Some airlines kind enough to let you smoke

Aeroflot is one of few airlines operating in Europe that still allows smoking on its aircraft. When US President Bill Clinton declared that all passenger flights into or out of the United States had to be smoke-free, the Russian airline protested that he was intruding into the economic activities of foreign companies outside the US and took the case to the International Air Transport Association.

Other airlines which permit smoking include **Royal Jordanian**, **Egyptair Emirates** and **Olympic**, but not on all routes. On some long-haul routes, **Air France** has installed smoking booths that expel smoke from the plane rather than let it circulate round the cabin.

Pilots with the Spanish airline, **Iberia**, have refused to stop smoking in the cockpit, claiming that a ban by the airline was an infringement of their rights. Truly desperate passengers could knock on the door of the cockpit and ask the pilot for a drag.

1997. Having asked for a non-smoking seat, Mr Bagwell lost his temper when passengers lit up in the smoking section in front of him. He became abusive towards passengers and staff, and eventually barged onto the flight deck at a critical moment in the plane's ascent. He was arrested on arrival at Heathrow and spent Christmas in jail.

Snigger if you will, but for every John Bagwell, there is a Scott Stevens, an Australian plumber forced to pay £400 for smoking in the toilets of an aircraft flying from Kenya to Gatwick in March 1998. Before lighting up he covered the smoke detector with paper towels, but they fell off as he was smoking. Staff escorted him back to his seat and he, too, was arrested on landing.

These rows only seem to blow up on long-haul flights, so some flight operators offer nicotine patches to smoking passengers, and others maintain smoking sections. But even these can give offence if they're not thought out in advance. One Hungarian airline thoughtfully placed smokers on the left hand side of the plane and was astonished to still receive complaints from non-smokers sitting on the right.

A terrible duty is born

Now that the one saving grace of air travel — the opportunity to pick up some cut-price fags in the duty free — has been abolished on EU internal flights, foreign holidays have become altogether less attractive.

The ban is unlikely to have any great effect on overall consumption. Before July 1999, just 1% of cigarettes smoked in the EU were sold at duty-free outlets. It doesn't sound like much, but godammit it was the cheapest 1%. It was also the bribe for the person whose house you stayed in for nothing, the returning gift for a sweetheart, and the fags-on-tap supply that kept you away from the local chokers — for the first week of your break anyway.

The solution seems to be to take your holidays outside the EU. But bear in mind that British and Irish airports' duty-free shops are among the most expensive in the world — sometimes more than twice the price of those abroad (see straw poll below).

If you're travelling to far-off lands and want to pick up cheap fags on the way, it's better not to buy them as you leave your home airport. Duty-free may well cost more than retail prices in your country of arrival. And if you're stopping or changing aircraft at other major airports such as Frankfurt or Dubai, it's also worth the wait.

If you can't resist buying them at the outset, at least try to wait till you're on the plane, where duty-free purchases are usually cheaper (though one major British airline charges even more than at airports).

Many duty-free shops have websites advertising their prices, allowing you to suss out the best deals in advance. The variety in the prices quoted below indicate that it's worth shopping around.

Airports	**Price of 200 Marlboro**
London, UK	€27.79 (Stg£16.99)
Dublin, Ireland	€20.98 (IR£16.20)
Frankfurt, Germany	€18.50
Split, Croatia	€14.60
Larnaca, Cyprus	€14.25
Auckland, New Zealand	€13.25
Bahrain	€13.00

Some famous smokers who, for one reason or another, are mostly dead

Che Guevara RIP 1928-1967

The lengths people will go to for a smoke occasionally fall nothing short of genius. Take Ernesto 'Che' Guevara, hero of the Cuban revolution and icon of student bedsits. Ironically, the first ambition of this cigar smoker's idol was to become a doctor and discover a cure for asthma, which afflicted him throughout his life.

Che began smoking only when he arrived in Cuba as part of the rebel force which overthrew the dictator Batista and installed Fidel Castro as leader. At one point, his medical condition became so bad that pulmonary emphysema set in. Doctors advised him to stop smoking, but the rebel leader persuaded them to allow him one cigar a day. He then arranged to have an extra-long cigar rolled for him, so that he could smoke all day without violating the agreement.

He went to an early grave, but not because of his passion for smoking. Rather, Guevara was shot while leading a peasant uprising in Bolivia in 1967.

Walter Raleigh 1552-1618

As a schoolboy I knew three things about Sir Walter Raleigh: he brought the potato from the New World; he threw his cloak down for Queen Elizabeth to walk on; and he brought tobacco to Britain. It turns out they're all untrue. (Go on, next you'll be telling me Raleigh didn't invent the bicycle either.) There was tobacco in Britain before Raleigh visited the New World, though he did sponsor some of the expeditions which brought back the first stores. Likewise the potato. The yarn about him spreading his cloak over a puddle is apocryphal.

Raleigh did, however, popularise the habit of smoking. He had great influence with Queen Elizabeth, and was something of a trend-setter at court. So when he began smoking, the practice spread among courtiers and, through them, the people of the land.

He was less popular at the court of Elizabeth's successor, James I, a fierce opponent of tobacco who wrote in his *Counterblaste to Tobacco* that smoking was "a custom loathsome to the eye, repulsive to the nose, dangerous to the braine". Raleigh soon fell foul of the new king, who eventually ordered his execution. He was beheaded in the Tower of London, but up to the moment of the chop, Raleigh refused to take his pipe from his mouth. It was duly removed, but not before his head.

8 Coughing up for your country
THE PRICE OF SMOKING

"Passive smokers, people too mean to buy their own cigarettes, are parasites who should be shunned and obliged to pay a special tax."
Brendan Glacken, writing in The Irish Times

There are a few occasions every year when smokers start to make noises about giving up: New Year, No-Smoking Day, the beginning of Lent. And then there are times when they seriously contemplate it. Like Budget Day.

On this day there's a show of solidarity, as addicts gather in the pubs and smoking rooms of the world to complain to sympathetic ears about the annual tax increases on booze and fags. Solemn vows of abstinence are taken, and defiant promises of continuation made — often by the same people at opposite ends of the day.

At present, well over three-quarters of the money you pay for a box of cigarettes goes straight to the government, and although British and Irish smokers pay the highest rates of tobacco tax in Europe, the levy is unlikely to go down, for several reasons.

Price and tax on 20 cigarettes

	Price	Tax
Britain	€7.22 (Stg£4.33)	79.5%
Ireland	€4.87 (IR£3.84)	78.1%
France	€3.35	76%
Belgium	€2.89	74.1%
Spain	€1.77	71.2%

Price of most popular brand in July 2001. Source: Tobacco Manufacturers' Association

For starters, it's extremely lucrative. Tobacco taxes bring in between £7 billion and £10 billion a year in the UK, enough to fund the British home office, foreign office, and agriculture ministry combined. And even though some smokers quit in response to the budgetary price hikes, the net tax gain means that the government still makes a profit. Furthermore this "sin tax" is uniquely popular among voters — even some smokers support it.

Cigarette tax increases have long been advocated by anti-smoking groups as one of the most effective ways of encouraging people to either give up or cut down. For every 2% added to the price of tobacco, consumption is supposed to drop by 1%. So theoretically, raising cigarette prices should be responsible for thousands of people quitting.

Price rises are also thought to have most impact among low-income groups and teenagers — the very smokers who are least

THE PRICE OF SMOKING

responsive to government warnings and health campaigns.

However, it seems public health is not the main motivation for the tobacco tax. If it were, governments would long ago have taxed it to the level of a luxury product, consumed only occasionally, and with considerably less damage to us all. After all, cigarettes are only truly dangerous because we can afford to buy them in quantities large enough to do serious harm.

All this for nothing

Trouble is, as we've paid more and more for cigarettes, the twin aims of reducing smoking and increasing tax have not materialised. Smoking levels have at least remained static, and the tax take from tobacco has fallen.

Why hasn't the theory worked in practice? Well, it's largely because the rules have been changed.

People don't want to pay high prices for cigarettes, but they'll pay low ones if they can. Britain and Ireland are now two of the most expensive countries in Europe in which to be a smoker, and the discrepancy in price between them and their neighbours has created a huge market in smuggled cigarettes.

Not only is the black market depriving the governments of billions of pounds a year in tax, it's also making smoking cheaper, which means the intended drop in consumption hasn't materialised. In fact, because sales of contraband cigarettes can't be monitored, smoking could actually be increasing without anybody knowing.

The smuggle bubble

By its nature, smuggling is hard to quantify, but the highest estimates are that one-third of all cigarettes smoked worldwide are contraband. In Britain alone during the 1990s, smuggling is thought to have increased fourfold. Smoking groups say it now accounts for 25% of all cigarettes smoked in the country, while customs officials say 20%, and cigarette companies say less than 10%.

Smuggling occurs on a small and large scale, from an individual hopping on a ferry with a suitcase full of tobacco, to huge containers crossing continents under false documentation. About three-quarters of the illegal traffic, though, is organised container fraud.

Europe is a central hub of the international cigarette trade, the base for shipments from America to eastern Europe and north Africa. Every day, truckloads of cigarettes make journeys by land and sea, crossing national borders and dipping in and out of the EU via Switzerland and Andorra. Amid a bewildering network of trade routes and border regulations, it is easy for a shipment to disappear.

For criminals, cigarettes present a golden opportunity. They are easy to transport in small or large volumes, and because of the large amount of tax involved, they offer a higher profit margin than most products.

In Ireland, for example, the pre-tax price of 20 cigarettes is a little over £1. The retail price is almost £4. By selling each box for, say, £2.50, a smuggler can substantially undercut the retail price and still make a huge profit.

Big business

But there are more than just criminals involved. The tobacco industry itself — while denying any involvement in smuggling and claiming it can do nothing to prevent it — benefits greatly from the illegal trade.

Flooding a market with cheap cigarettes keeps the crucial low-income smokers smoking and counters the effect of tax increases. Furthermore, the loss of considerable tax revenue due to the abundance of low-cost cigarettes on the black market makes a convincing case for reducing the official price of cigarettes. This scenario actually arose in Canada; when prices rose and smuggling became widespread, the tax on tobacco was slashed to combat it.

Tobacco firms lose nothing from the black market. They make the same profit from smuggled cigarettes as from those sold through conventional channels. Because they sell the product before it enters the smuggling chain, they are quite happy to sell cigarettes to dealers who are known to flog them on to smugglers.

Industry memos made public during litigation show that some of the world's biggest cigarette companies have not only facilitated illegal trade, but have deliberately used it as a branding and promotional tactic.

Cigarette companies knowingly provide the first link in the contraband chain. Many of the cigarettes smuggled into Britain and Ireland are actually manufactured there in the first place. The companies produce huge volumes of brands which are smoked only in these markets and designate them for export to countries where

Get yourself some bootleg

It is obviously completely illegal to deal in smuggled goods. This publication hereby decries the practice and advocates that you poison your body with legitimate, duty-paid, barely affordable tobacco products only. But let's imagine that, for argument's sake, you wanted to buy some of the ones that find their way into the country by illicit routes. How would you go about it?

- Take an imaginary trip to one of the ports of northern France, where cigarettes are about half what they cost in Britain or Ireland. Britons could also travel to Adinkerke, Belgium, one of the nerve centres of the clandestine tobacco trade.
- About £100 million worth of cigarettes are illegally brought into Britain every year. This contraband is available through door-to-door transactions, sales in private houses, and a brisk street trade in shopping districts. Have a hypothetical conversation with the local dodgy person to discover the outlet nearest you.
- Log on one of the foreign websites selling cheap cigarettes. A, um, chap I know very well ordered 200 Marlboro Lights for €29 from **www.smokeplanet.com** and 200 from **www.smokefarm.com** for 40% less than they would have cost in Ireland. Three weeks later, both packages arrived together, apparently from the same address in Spain. Nice price, but you wouldn't want to be gasping for a fag. Customs have been known to confiscate packages. If they find out.

Make that early grave pay

Smokers are forever being told about the cost of their habit: £1,500 a year if you smoke 20 a day.

Now, while I don't doubt that you're a devil-may-care, laugh-in-the-face-of-death smoker who wouldn't let monetary concerns get in the way of sensual pleasure, I presume also that, like most people, you have something of a split personality. So if you occasionally worry about your health, your weight, and even — once in a blue moon — the sordid matter of coin, then it may interest you to know that smoking has the odd financial benefit.

Though insurance firms generally penalise smokers for their unhealthful habit, some institutions will actually pay higher annuity rates to those who state that they have smoked at least ten cigarettes a day for the past ten years.

Briefly, an annuity means that you pay a lump sum to an insurance company and they guarantee you a monthly or yearly income until you die. The logic is that, since smokers die younger than non-smokers, they will draw on their annuity for a shorter period. And you don't have to keep smoking to collect on the policy — you can give up as soon as you buy the annuity.

In recent years, long life expectancies have been chipping away at the returns on annuities. If this trend continues, smoking may be the only way to guarantee yourself a happy retirement.

nobody has ever heard of them — so-called "phantom" markets. As soon as they leave the country, they disappear, only to be smuggled back in without duty having been paid on them.

In the 1990s, exports from the UK to Andorra of brands popular only in Britain and Ireland rocketed. Either Andorra had become overnight a nation of chain-smoking Anglophiles, or the cigarettes were secretly finding their way back into these countries. When customs officers cracked down on the Andorra connection, the exports shifted to Montenegro. It and other Balkan states, along with Cyprus, Belgium and Luxembourg, are now the main phantom markets for cigarettes smuggled into Britain and Ireland.

Smuggling has also been used by tobacco multinationals as an "entry strategy" into new markets. In China, for example, the sale of Marlboro, Camel and other international brands is restricted because of the threat they pose to the established local market. Smuggling international brands into the country for unofficial sale at knock-down prices draws smokers away from the local cigarettes and "builds the brand" in the new market.

Eventually, the local manufacturer is forced to admit multinationals into the official marketplace to stop the black-market price from undercutting the locals.

Some famous smokers who, for one reason or another, are mostly dead

Winston Churchill RIP 1874-1965

There is, in every smoker's life, a semi-mythical figure of an older generation who smoked huge numbers of filterless cigarettes, cigars or pipes right up to the day they died, at a ripe old age, of a headcold while tobagganing down Mount Everest, having just scaled it for the fifth time.

The person is usually a relative, thus genetically linking their robust constitution to the smoker's. In the absence of such a relative, however, the smoker wishing to see off a sanctimonious health nut in an argument can always cite one of the great freaks of nature who smoked all their long life at no apparent cost to their health. Winston Churchill, almost the human embodiment of a cigar, is one of these. Whisky guzzler, wit, war hero, intellectual and nonagenarian, Churchill has many of the qualities that are best in smokers.

Still, you may be sorry to learn — especially if your opponent in the argument already knows it — that Churchill smoked little in later life. By the start of his second term as prime minister in the early 1950s, a fierce cough had forced him to cut out smoking almost completely. But he wanted to preserve the image of the invincible old bulldog, either for political reasons or out of vanity, so he always kept an unlit cigar in his mouth. He even carried a half-smoked cigar in his pocket and stuck it in his mouth whenever a photographer appeared.

This moderation in Churchill's twilight years might help explain his longevity, which until recently was — as the man himself might have said — a riddle wrapped in a mystery, inside an enigma.

The Spice Girls
Born 1995

Winston persuaded the world he smoked when he didn't — The Spice Girls had the opposite aim. Back in the days when they had a huge teenage fan-base, the girls used to deny that they smoked, even though the media reported Emma Bunton (who as a schoolgirl appeared on an anti-smoking poster), Victoria Beckham (ten a day after Brooklyn was born), and Mel B indulging. Estranged Spice Geri Halliwell was denounced by anti-smoking groups in 1999 for smoking in public while also supporting a breast-cancer awareness campaign. Melanie Chisholm, being Sporty, was always Smoke-free Spice. At least I now understand that crypto-lyric: "I wanna really really really wanna ciggie cigar".

9 *Publicity Wars*
SELLING CIGARETTES

"The cigarette industry has been artfully maintaining that cigarette advertising has nothing to do with total sales ... I am always amused by the suggestion that advertising, a function that has been shown to increase consumption of virtually every other product, somehow miraculously fails to work for tobacco products."
Emerson Foote, former CEO of McCann-Erickson advertising

Tobacco is far more a marketing industry than a manufacturing one. Cigarettes are easy to make, consisting only of tobacco, paper and filter and, removed from their distinctive boxes, they all look pretty much the same. So to flog one brand over another, companies need to market like mad. They beguile their followers with attractive phrases and popular mythologies, and win loyalty with clear, memorable imagery.

This imagery is part of every smoker's consciousness. I have clear memories of ads for every brand of cigarette I have ever smoked — a man in khakis on a raft smoking Camels, a golden sunset with a Benson & Hedges logo at its centre, and Silk Cut's purple poodle.

The Marlboro Cowboy ads are widely credited as the most

successful ad campaign of all time for any product. This ingenuity in cigarette advertising is driven partly by competition between brands, but also by constant restrictions on tobacco marketing.

In Britain in the 1980s, the tobacco industry agreed to new advertising restrictions which forbade depiction of smoking in a glamorous light. There followed a series of abstract advertisements that defied analysis by enforcement agencies but used provocative imagery (chopped up silk etc) to drive home their messages.

Cigarette makers insist they have a right to "talk to their customers" through advertising, to woo them from one brand to another. "We don't advertise to recruit smokers. We advertise to encourage adult smokers of other brands to try ours, and to encourage brand loyalty among those adults who already smoke our brands," said Philip Morris in 1996.

Anti-smoking activists say you can't sell the brand without selling the product, and that the real purpose of cigarette marketing is to sell the habit to non-smokers, especially young non-smokers. They're backed up, as ever, by the tobacco industry's own internal memos.

The 1988 marketing plan of Imperial Tobacco Canada outlines a more likely version of the industry's strategy: "If the last ten years have taught us anything, it is that the industry is dominated by the companies who respond most to the needs of younger smokers. Our efforts on these brands will remain on maintaining their relevance to smokers in these younger groups."

The health lobby wants to see a ban on tobacco advertising in as many countries as possible, which, it believes, will have a marked effect on smoking. It quotes a wealth of research in support of the ban, and insists it will reduce smoking rates by up to 16%.

That may be a little too optimistic. Smoking has not decreased in Ireland since tobacco ads were banned. Italy and Portugal also imposed bans, only to see smoking increase as a price war between brands forced cigarette prices down. And Russians smoked heavily for years under the Communist regime, when there was no advertising. In France, on the other hand, teenage smoking quickly reduced by 15% after advertising and sponsorship were banned.

> ### Smoking in the press
>
> If the influence of a tobacco ad ban on cigarette consumption is uncertain, its effect on the media is easier to predict. Smokers can expect more negative coverage of the tobacco industry, and an increase in health information. Until now elements of the British press have been slow to criticise their advertising paymasters, from whom they receive £50 million a year in tobacco ads.

After these commercials ...

And tobacco marketers are always quick to exploit cracks in the regulations. One method of alternative marketing by tobacco companies is "brand stretching": the creation of commodities such as the Marlboro Classic clothing line or Camel shoes and watches.

Another tactic is loyalty schemes, in which smokers of a particular

Tobacco ads — the haves and the have-nots

Europe comes the heavy ...
An EU directive banning tobacco advertising and sponsorship throughout the community was formally adopted in 1998. It also restricted advertising in shops, and advertising of other products carrying tobacco logos, such as Camel boots and watches.

... then wimps out
But the directive was overturned before it came into practice, following legal challenges by the tobacco industry and by Germany, which runs one of the world's biggest tobacco companies. A watered-down version is now on the agenda.

While Britain fiddles ...
A Tobacco Advertising and Promotion Bill, broadly following the spirit of the first EU directive, has been published but has yet to go through parliament. Banning tobacco advertising has been on the agenda of the British government since 1997.

... and some of us are just perfect
Some of us are very organised altogether, and already have laws which ban advertising of tobacco products. The squeaky clean list includes Ireland, Belgium, Denmark, Finland, France, Italy, Portugal and Sweden.

cigarette collect vouchers entitling them to gifts. The gifts are usually typical youth-market paraphernalia — scooters, clubbing holidays and cameras — although a Benson & Hedges scheme in 1996 offered a free baby cot if you collected wrappers equivalent to 50 cigarettes a day over nine months. Nice.

The latest proposals from the EU would ban advertising in areas where it is currently popular — the press and outdoor hoardings — but allow it to continue in the tobacco trade press and on websites selling tobacco. The Internet is likely to be used for cheap direct mailing and other sales campaigns. Tobacco trade magazines could become a lucrative publishing niche overnight.

Future marketing could also see more product placement in film, computer games and fashion shoots, and the extension of direct mail. All in all, it's unlikely you've seen the last of the cigarette ad.

Sports sponsorship: they think it's all over ...

When television advertising of tobacco products was banned in 1965, cigarette companies immediately looked around for new ways to promote their products on TV. Before long they began to sponsor televised sporting events, which worked so well that by the end of the decade they were daubing cigarette logos on helmets, lawns, cars, and just about anything that moved in a sporting arena.

In pursuit of maximum TV exposure, the tobacco industry especially targeted long-duration games, so that some pretty boring sports — cricket, darts, bowls, snooker — became the grateful recipients of large amounts of sponsorship.

Over the years, complicity developed between tobacco firms and broadcasters, who would ensure the company's logo appeared in shots during crucial moments in play. ("They think it's all over ... oh just look at that hoarding behind the goal", that sort of thing.) In 1992, a BBC report found that cigarette logos were so ubiquitous in televised sports, that the organisation was broadcasting the

Fag boxes on wheels

The sponsorship paid to the average bowls tournament might just about buy a new set of tyres for a grand prix vehicle. Glamorous, dangerous, and watched by a global TV audience of 400 million people, Formula 1 is the perfect vehicle for cigarette promotion. Tobacco's £170 million in annual sponsorship literally fuels the sport.

The sponsors make every penny pay. A racing car's visible surface is divided among the backers with micro-precision. The primary sponsor — Camel, Marlboro or Benson & Hedges — chooses the background colours and usually the conspicuous nose-cone and cockpit spots. The remaining surface area is left to the minor sponsors, on the understanding that their logos appear in smaller type than the main backers.

TV cameras focus only on the leading cars in a race, so sponsors have to make sure their teams have the best of everything in order that their brands achieve maximum exposure. Top teams such as Ferrari or McLaren can earn up to $50 million a year from tobacco benefactors.

equivalent of several tobacco ads per hour. Being banned from TV advertising was arguably the best thing that had ever happened to tobacco promoters.

Now, tobacco sponsorship is also facing the chop. Along with advertising, it has already been banned once by the EU, only for the law to be repealed. It's unlikely to escape so easily a second time, as British legislation in the pipeline plans to outlaw sports sponsorship by 2006. When the crunch comes, the financiers of the Benson & Hedges Cricket Trophy will find themselves on a sticky wicket. Snooker bosses, accustomed to £10 million a year from Regal, Embassy and Benson & Hedges, will be forced fill their pockets elsewhere. And darts — not to put too fine a point on it — could hit the wall altogether.

Major sports such as Formula 1, cricket and snooker should be able to attract alternative sponsors, but bowls, angling, greyhound racing and darts might find it tougher. After all, most companies in search of TV exposure can simply buy conventional advertising spots. Few are as desperate as cigarette manufacturers to promote their merchandise through sponsorship.

The silver-screen salesforce

Some of the world's top cigarette promoters have never received a penny from the tobacco industry, though the publicity they have generated for the habit is second-to-none. The great screen smokers — Humphrey Bogart, Bette Davis, Barbara Stanwyck — all coolly drawing on fat, filterless cigarettes, have arguably done more for tobacco sales than any amount of conventional advertising.

Smoking is a useful creative tool for filmmakers, giving characters more character and props departments fewer headaches. It makes *Die Hard* Bruce Willis a man of the people, Sandra Bullock a bad girl, and Arnold Schwarzenegger a human being (except when he's playing a machine). Even more often, it simply gives actors something to do with their hands.

But it's not all art for art's sake. Filmmakers are only too glad to accept cash gifts in return for a bit of product placement. Cigarette industry documents from the 1970s and 1980s reveal a regular, multi-million dollar trade between a top tobacco multinational and Hollywood studios.

In one memo, Sylvester Stallone agrees to use certain tobacco products in five films for $500,000. In another, a cigarette company offers £70,000 if its billboards are used as part of a movie set. A third document reveals that filming Martin Sheen smoking Marlboro throughout *Apocalypse Now* netted the producers millions of dollars.

Though smoking is far less popular now than it was in 1950s, its prominence in movies has not diminished. A US reporter surveying the top films in American theatres in one week in the late 1990s found only one without a smoking scene: a Disney cartoon. In other films, specific products like Camel, Marlboro and Winston were given an airing, and cigar smoking featured in half the movies.

Children's movies are no exception. Philip Morris documents from the 1980s show lists of films in which the company placed tobacco products. They include *Who Framed Roger Rabbit?* and *The Muppet Movie.* Apart from the movie titles, the only other data on the sheets were the age limits. Nearly all were Regular, Parental Guidance or 13 certificates.

With so much huffing and puffing on screen, a two-hour movie in a smoke-free cinema can be quite an endurance test for the committed smoker.

The health lobby strikes back

Cigarette companies are such infamous exponents of hard-sell advertising that it is easy to forget they are only one side in the propaganda war that rages around tobacco. In fact, they look more like the losers every day; as their promotional opportunities diminish, anti-smoking messages receive more exposure than ever.

Health promotion groups now mount expensive ad campaigns, produce leaflets and literature, and host sophisticated websites proclaiming the hazards of cigarettes and the wickedness of their makers. Time, effort and cash are also spent spreading the anti-smoking message through newspapers and other media.

Although the marketing budgets of cigarette companies still dwarf the sums devoted to anti-smoking campaigns, this disparity masks the fact that the anti-smoking lobby gets a lot of free publicity. Voluntary support from the medical profession is widespread, and ever since nicotine replacement products have come on the market, the pharmaceutical industry has spent a lot of money persuading the public that smoking is bad. Occasionally, the tobacco industry itself foots the bill, as with the "government" health warning it prints on every box of cigarettes.

What's more, the warnings are about to become more prominent. At present, the textual warning occupies around 4% of the surface of a cigarette packet. In 2003, under an EU law, this will increase to 30%. The new warnings will be couched in supposedly more direct language ("Smoking kills" or "Smoking seriously harms others around you, especially children"), and the allotted area may include photos or graphics, to compete with the eye-catching cigarette packaging.

The EU Commissioner for Social Affairs expects these measures will help reduce European smoking rates from one in three adults to one in five. I wonder.

Death? We'll buy that

I mean, health warning, what health warning? Like most smokers, I have become blind to the two centimetres of black-on-white type at the bottom of my cigarette box. If a new phrase appears there, as it does about every 10 years, I read it but continue smoking. Since the warning itself is patently true, I form subconscious objections to its po-faced wording, its predictability, and its obvious exclusions. Smoking while pregnant may harm your baby, but it may not. Smoking causes cancer, but not for everyone. After a while, the warning sort of stops being there.

The introduction of health messages on cigarette boxes was a voluntary action by tobacco companies in the early 1970s, a disclaimer in case someone sued them for knowingly selling a dangerous product. The marketing wizards of Big Tobacco would hardly have made that kind of decision if it were going to put a serious dent in smoking rates.

Perhaps a photo of a pair of diseased lungs on my cigarette box will have a different effect. Or perhaps not. One thing that makes me doubt it is the sales record of Death Cigarettes. In the early 1990s, the Enlightened Tobacco Company began to make and sell Death Cigarettes.

"Smoking does not make you sexy, stylish or sophisticated. It kills you," trumpeted the Death packs, which were jet black except for stark white lettering and a large skull and crossbones on the front. "We are not selling a pack of lies, we are selling a pack of cigarettes. Death™ is a responsible way to market a legally available consumer product which kills people when used exactly as intended." Smokers bought Death in droves, helped by a rock-bottom pack price.

The cigarettes have since been banned by a European court over the company's cut-price sales policy, but their promotion showed that smokers react better to a bit of candid originality than to a health warning that amounts to little more than a dare.

To a hardened smoker, a scarier warning only ups the challenge inherent in smoking. A 700% bigger warning equals 700% bigger health risk, equals 700% more coolness if you continue to smoke. For better or for worse, that's the way a lot of people see it.

Oh what a handy war

Imagine yourself in 1915, in a trench somewhere along the Somme, composing a bit of last-minute war poetry with the lads. In a few minutes your sergeant-major's going to whip out a revolver and order you to hop over the top or be finished off by him. Someone offers you a cigarette. Do you say: "No thanks, it might cause me impaired circulation in late middle-age"? Not likely.

Hale and hearty twilight years don't count for much on the battlefield, so it's not surprising that war has been the cigarette industry's most effective marketing tool.

Britain's first cigarette manufacturer, Robert Gloag, saw the commercial potential of cigarettes in the Crimea during the war in the 1850s. The Turkish, French and Russian soldiers were all avid cigarette smokers, and the British soon took to the new product.

By the outbreak of World War I in 1914, mechanised production had made cigarettes more viable, and the four years that followed saw a generation of young men take to the habit.

Cigarettes suited soldiers. Unlike a pipe, they could be smoked on the march, and in economies made meaningless by war, they doubled up as currency. For people far from home, living with chronic suffering in impossible conditions, cigarettes were the nearest thing to a luxury. Plus, they came in handy for torture.

Their value was recognised by General Pershing when America

entered the war. His desperate message to Washington read: "You ask what we need to win this war. We need tobacco, more tobacco — even more than food." He got it. The general's request was answered by RJ Reynolds, which reassured the soldiers that "the Camels are coming".

The next time the world went to war, several other US companies saw the marketing opportunity. Wrigleys supplied chewing gum to troops, and Mars and Hershey convinced the generals that chocolate was an important energy food that should be included in all soldiers' rations. The army went chocolate crazy, but smoking reached new highs too. Between 1939 and 1945, smoking in Britain increased by 150% among men and fourfold among women. Cigarettes were also included in the rations of American GIs, and President Roosevelt, noting tobacco's positive effect on morale, declared it a protected crop. By the end of the war, smoking in the US was at an all-time high.

Some famous smokers who, for one reason or another, are mostly dead

Napoleon Bonaparte RIP
1769-1821

The Little Corporal was not a smoker, but like today's governments, he was happy to draw income from tobacco and tolerated the habit in others. Early on he realised that smokers would smoke no matter what tax he put on the tobacco, and later he used the income from the crop to finance his wars.

Napoleon's own contribution to the imperial coffers was considerable; at the height of his reign he put a massive seven pounds of snuff a month up his nose and during his exile on St Helena upped his consumption even further.

His pragmatic attitude to smoking was well expressed by his nephew and namesake Napoleon III who, when asked to ban smoking, replied: "I will forbid this vice at once, as soon as you can name a virtue that brings in as much revenue." Would that today's politicians could match his candour.

Shane Warne
Born 1969

On New Year's Day, 1999, cricketer Shane Warne made a resolution most people could only dream of. The Australian vice-captain — well known as a 40-a-day smoker — had struck a deal with the Nicorette chewing gum manufacturer Upjohn & Pharmacia to stay off tobacco for four months in return for Aus$200,000 (€105,000).

No pressure now Shane, but if you smoke before the time's up, you can kiss the cash goodbye. I think you can probably guess what happened next.

Three months and 25 days later, Warne was seen smoking in a bar in the West Indies. Remembering the highly publicised prize, he mounted the defence of Shaggy: "It wasn't me." When photographic proof was produced, his memory returned. Oh yeah, that's right, I did actually smoke one cigarette that night. Sorry everybody. Sorry Upjohn & Pharmacia.

Well, what's a sponsor to do? Take the money back and admit that Nicorette didn't work? No, luckily for Warne, the sponsors were more image-conscious than he was. They described the incident as a once-off, and insisted he kept every penny of the $200,000.

Wasn't it odd that Warne should have had his one and only moment of weakness in full public glare? Shock horror, a year later during a match in New Zealand, the cricketer had to be restrained by police from attacking a teenager who had photographed him smoking a cigarette. Just the one, I'm sure.

10 Smokers — the premier league

TARGET MARKETING

"We don't smoke this shit. We just sell it. We reserve the right to smoke for the young, the poor, the black and the stupid."
Model Dave Goerlitz paraphrasing the Winston ad team

Some kinds of people smoke more than others. If you're young, poor, black, female or gay, you're on the tobacco industry's hit-list, and if you fit all five descriptions, you're the target of some pretty heavy marketing.

The youth of today

One summer, midway through adolescence, I took a moment off from being the self-righteous little twerp who wittered on about the dangers of smoking and stamped gleefully on adults' discarded cigarette butts, and instead took a bite of the forbidden fruit.

When I returned to school in September, I noticed that lots of lads who just three months previously had been the class "squares", "knobs" and "queers" were now ingratiating themselves with the coolest boys in the school simply by starting to smoke. Taking note of this golden ticket to social-acceptance Wonkaland, I resolved to walk the three miles home at the end of the day, and spent my busfare on ten Camels. Fifteen years on, I'm still trying to quit.

Heard the story before? Give or take a few details, it's the experience of nearly every smoker's initiation into the habit. Almost 90% of smokers begin as teenagers, when bodily fallibility is not much in evidence and we consider ourselves impervious to disease, ageing and addiction. By the time we realise that smoking is doing some damage, we're hooked.

Since three million smokers die around the world every year, cigarette companies are under constant pressure to win new recruits. They know that if they can induct a young person into smoking, there is a good chance that person will reward them with several decades of cigarette purchases. On the other hand, if that person reaches age 20 without smoking, they are unlikely ever to begin.

Though tobacco firms claim their advertising focuses on promoting one cigarette brand over others, the evidence is overwhelming that popularising youth smoking is a central strategy. A memo from Philip Morris, makers of Marlboro, sums up the industry's marketing strategy: "The ability to attract new smokers and develop them into a young adult franchise is key to brand development."

A favourite sales strategy is to paint smoking as an adult habit. In the 1970s, a tobacco advertising executive encouraged copywriters at his agency to: "To the best of your ability, (considering some legal constraints), relate the cigarette to pot, wine, beer, sex, etc."

In fairness, children could probably make this association on their own, and there's more to child smoking than advertising. After all, the number of teenagers who smoke tobacco is similar to the number who smoke dope, which occurs in the absence of any advertising. At an age when smoking a cigarette falls somewhere between a dare and a boast, peer pressure also plays a crucial role. For girls, the fear of gaining weight can be a prime motivation.

But the role of marketing should not be underestimated either. One study has found that boys whose favourite sport was grand prix racing were twice as likely to become regular smokers than those who had no interest in the sport. The mere presence of ads in mainstream media also legitimises smoking as an acceptable social norm. As long as the kids keep smoking, the tills keep ringing.

The second sex — just about

Targeted marketing of cigarettes to women began in the late 1920s, when Philip Morris pitched its new cigarette, Marlboro, complete with red tip to hide lipstick marks, at the female consumer.

It didn't catch on, but when Lucky Strike ads started emphasising the slimming benefits of cigarettes ("Reach for a Lucky instead of a sweet"), women took to the habit like suffragettes to railings. By the end of World War II, 40% of women in the UK and 33% in America were smokers.

Modern cigarette marketing still emphasises the slimming theme

Women's movement

Not many larfs in this little aside, I'm afraid. Smoking is taking its toll on female health.

Apart from lung cancer (which in 1987 overtook breast cancer as the leading cancer in US women), heart disease (the top killer of women in the first world) and the plethora of other ailments which affect all smokers, women who smoke are also more susceptible to cervical cancer. For women on the Pill, smoking increases their risk of stroke and heart disease by a factor of 10.

(note the preponderance of the words "Slim" and "Lights"), and has added that of sexual independence. In the 1960s, "You've come a long way, Baby" was the launch slogan for Virginia Slims, a cigarette designed specifically for women. Since then, there has been a profusion of cigarettes aimed at women, including the many low-tar, low-nicotine brands, which are particularly popular with better-off women.

Smoking among women declined between the 1970s and the 1990s, but a hardcore of around 26% of British women have refused to kick the habit. Overall, women are still "the second sex", but only just. In Ireland, 28% of females smoke, compared with 29% of males, and the rate of female smoking is falling more slowly. Young, fashion-conscious females make up the highest proportion of smokers, and women with eating disorders are more likely to smoke.

Women say it is harder for them to give up. A 1999 British report with the eye-catching title *Sex and Smoking*, showed that women are less determined to quit than men. The researchers concluded that women had a greater emotional attachment to cigarettes: 44% of female smokers named smoking as their greatest pleasure, compared with 38% of men.

Nothing demonstrates this attachment to cigarettes better than the statistics on pregnant smokers. Despite the well-documented health consequences (premature birth; more miscarriages and stillbirths; damage to the child's mental and physical development; and sudden infant death syndrome), around one-third of women who are with child, are also "with fags". Of those who do quit while pregnant, one fifth relapse during pregnancy and nearly all are smoking again one year after the birth.

If women are the old reliables for tobacco companies in the western world, they are also their great hope in developing markets. Of the 800 million smokers in the developing world, just 100 million are women, leaving a huge untapped market.

In the southern hemisphere and eastern Europe, tobacco firms are once again selling smoking as a modern, emancipatory habit for the next generation of women, with considerable success. If the current rate of uptake continues, by 2024 20% of women in the developing world will smoke.

As smoking-related diseases continue to afflict women, the lifespan gap between the sexes is shrinking, and the two could soon be on a par. In the words of the US Surgeon General: "Women who smoke like men die like men." Equality at last.

It's a black thing

In times of infirmity I'm sometimes drawn to mentholated cigarettes, because they taste like Vicks and must be good for me. But having ended up with a disproportionately high number of colds, chest complaints and sore throats, I know they're not the elixir I first imagined. As with "light" brands, menthol smokers tend to inhale more deeply because of the cooling effect of the flavouring. This can expose smokers of menthols to even greater levels of toxins and carcinogens than smokers of non-menthol cigarettes with comparable nicotine content.

Suddenly I'm glad I don't go for menthols as my regular brand. But some people smoke nothing else. Among their greatest devotees are blacks in the US, where three out four black smokers smoke menthol cigarettes.

Smoking patterns for black America are quite different to those for whites. Blacks start smoking later in life and go through fewer cigarettes per day. While black teenagers in the US smoke little, in adulthood they are one of the heaviest-smoking ethnic groups (27% of black American adults smoke, compared to 25% of whites and 20% of Hispanics).

Despite being late starters and relatively moderate consumers of cigarettes, black smokers' health suffers more. In the US, blacks have higher death rates from heart disease and stroke than whites, Asians Hispanics or native Americans. They are also at greater risk of dying from lung cancer: 81% of African-American men who smoke and have

	Black Caribbean	Indian	Pakistani	Bangladeshi	Chinese	Irish	Total pop.
% Men	35	23	26	44	17	39	27
% Women	25	6	5	1	9	33	27

Source: Health Survey for England 2000

Inhaling for England

In England, smoking rates vary among ethnic populations. Bangladeshis, Irish and Afro-Caribbeans are the heaviest smokers. Many in the heaviest-smoking groups live in inner-city ghettos where poverty and unemployment are high and educational standards low, so immigrant smoking may be quite different than for each race in its country of origin. Smoking rates among Irish people living in England, for example, are far higher than for Irish people in Ireland.

contracted lung cancer die from the disease, compared with 54% of white men.

With this high-risk health profile, you might think blacks deserve to be treated differently by the tobacco industry. Needless to say, they are. There is a long history of tobacco companies marketing menthol cigarettes to black smokers. In the 1960s, the Kool campaign, featuring a jazzy black penguin named Willie, helped make Kool the number one brand among black smokers, until it was replaced by Newport, another menthol, in the late 1980s. In the 1990s, Joe Camel was given a new, hip-hop image for the launch of Camel Menthol.

Black America was not just singled out for targeted advertising. It also benefited from the munificence of the cigarette industry, which has been a reliable employer of blacks, a source (often the only available source) of funds for civil rights groups and voter registration campaigns, and the paymaster for scholarships for black students. It has also supported black dance, arts and music (the Kool Jazz Festival is the best-known example). You don't need a degree in marketing to know that such philanthropy usually comes at a price.

Recognising this, black communities are organising and fighting back. In the past ten years, they have succeeded in getting the Uptown brand (a menthol, heavily marketed in black neighbourhoods) taken off the market. They also protested against the test-marketing of Marlboro Mild, a menthol brand made by Phillip Morris, in Atlanta, Georgia, where the population is 70% black. Presumably, the cigarette companies aren't picking up the tab for that campaign.

Nowt so queer as smokers

In recent years, cigarette companies eager to capture the so-called "pink pound" have joined the fashion, travel and design industries in targeting gays and lesbians. Marketers believe that this is a loyal and brand-conscious market, whose consumers favour brands that are

If you ain't broke ...

... then you're far less likely to smoke. Smokers share many traits, but the one feature we are most likely to have in common is poverty. In every city, in every country, and in every category of smoker, the poor out-smoke the rich. Hence, racial minorities — often the poorest in the society they inhabit — experience high rates of smoking. Women in Western society may be heavy smokers, but poorly educated, blue-collar women out-smoke their well-to-do sisters by four to one. The rich/poor divide also defines global smoking patterns. The prosperous West may be burdened with smoking-related illnesses, but it is home to only 100 million smokers, as against the developing world's 800 million. You wouldn't be poor for all the money in the world.

seen to support the gay community, either through advertising or other means — hence donations to AIDS charities and sponsorship of Gay Pride events by tobacco and drinks companies.

Gay rights groups in the US have pointed to campaigns for Benson & Hedges Special Kings, Marlboro, Montclair and Virginia Slims which they believe are aimed at gays or lesbians. This community, they say, has enough health problems without being singled out for special treatment by the tobacco industry.

About half of gay men smoke, compared with just over a quarter of all adult males, and research has confirmed high (though less marked) smoking rates among gay women.

Writing in *Tobacco Control,* Kevin Goebel contends that "the pressures that result in teenage smoking — self-esteem issues and the need for peer acceptance, the need for rebellion and liberation and the development of style and individuality — are compounded for lesbians, bisexuals, and gay men struggling with their sexuality." Many gays quote the bar culture — also responsible for a three-times-average rate of alcoholism among gays — as a factor in their smoking.

Awareness of the smoking issue has prompted some gay health groups, most of which began as AIDS charities, to run stop-smoking courses. A London group, Rubberstuffers, which made its name distributing free condoms, now points out that "gay men are more likely to die from smoking than HIV".

Some famous smokers who, for one reason or another, are mostly dead

Jeffrey Bernard RIP
1932-1997

A former *Spectator* columnist, Jeffrey Bernard, was famous for his uncompromising indulgence in smoking, drinking and sex, and his vivid descriptions of it in his column, Low Life, which was once described as "a suicide note in weekly instalments". His extraordinary lifestyle was the subject of a hit West End Play, *Jeffrey Bernard Is Unwell,* the name taken from the excuse line used by the *Spectator* when Bernard was too drunk to file copy.

In 1965, Bernard was diagnosed as having a diseased pancreas and advised to stop drinking. He continued. In 1991 he got gangrene, caused by bad circulation to the extremities, caused by smoking, and had a leg amputated. He went on smoking until the day he died. Odd that he managed to avoid AIDS, given his claim that he slept with over 500 women. Bernard is a sobering reminder of what excess can do to a person's body, but he is a hero to many who live life according to the maxim of Clement Freud: "If you give up smoking, drinking and loving, you don't actually live longer; it just seems longer."

Bernard died in relative obscurity of a heart attack, on the same day as Mother Theresa and six days after Princess Diana. He had always said it would be just his luck to go on the same day as the Queen Mother.

The Marlboro Man RIP
1941-1992

Marlboro, originally sold as a luxury brand in the 1920s, then marketed as a women's cigarette, was re-launched yet again as a mass-market product in the 1950s. The accompanying ad campaign, featuring a lone cowboy in rugged desert locations with the slogan "Come to Marlboro Country", is considered the most successful of all time, and made Marlboro the world's top-selling brand.

For the ads, Philip Morris employed a series of strong, square-jawed men. Dressed in buckskin jackets and blue jeans, they were photographed alone, on horseback, smoking cigarettes, with the craggy desert as backdrop. The images sold the themes of escapism, individuality, and timelessness, while the simple caption implied that Marlboro could deliver these qualities.

Wayne McLaren was an actor, rodeo rider and Hollywood stuntman before becoming one of the Marlboro men. The job involved lengthy filming and photography sessions, with regular retakes and constant lighting of fresh cigarettes. McLaren smoked 30 a day for about 25 years, before dying of lung cancer in 1992, aged 51. His last words were: "Tobacco will kill you, and I am living proof of it."

11 *You say tomato, I say tobacco*
THE SMOKER'S CHOICES

"I must be prompt over this matter ... It is quite a three-pipe problem, and I beg that you won't speak to me for fifty minutes."
Sherlock Holmes in The Red-Headed League,
by Sir Arthur Conan Doyle

Tobacco is a plant of the genus Nicotania, a genus of the nightshade family. Bet that means a lot to you. A botanist friend tells me that it's related to the tomato and the potato plants, but then botanists are always making such unlikely associations just to make their job sound interesting ("Did you know, the pansy is actually part of the triffid family? And grass is the same thing as rhubarb. Honestly!").

Anyway, this second-cousin-twice-removed of the tomato plant was first cultivated in central America 4,000 years ago by the Mayan civilisation, who smoked it in religious ceremonies. From there, it spread to other regions of the American continent and was taken up by other native American tribes.

When Columbus arrived in America in 1492, he observed the

natives smoking, chewing and taking snuff. On his return to Europe, he passed on the monstrous untruth that the people of India smoked like troopers, as he had no idea where he'd just been.

Subsequent European visitors to the Americas discovered a) where they were, and b) that pipe and cigar smoking were, indeed, widespread. Sailors and traders took up the habit and, in the century that followed, introduced it not just to their native lands, but to every far-flung region of the world. The first tobacco shipments arrived in Britain in 1585, and by the early 17th century, smoking had been practised in Russia, Germany, China and Japan.

The world's first commercial tobacco plantation was established by John Rolfe, husband of Pocahontas (he's not the guy in the film), in the English colony of Virginia in 1612. It proved so successful as a cash crop that cultivation spread throughout what are now the southeastern United States: Virginia, North and South Carolina, Florida, Georgia, Kentucky and Tennessee. This is still tobacco country, and the US is still one of the world's top three growers of the crop, alongside China and Brazil.

However, the plant thrives in a variety of soils and climates (it has even been produced on UK farms in the past) and is now grown in roughly 100 countries around the world. In Europe, Spain, Italy, Greece and Turkey are the major producers; in Africa, Zimbabwe and Malawi; in Asia, Japan and India.

The average plant is two to three metres tall, with around 40 large droopy leaves, which are the smokable part. There are several varieties of tobacco — burley, oriental, flue-cured, dark-fired and dark air cured — most taking their names from the method of drying the leaves after harvest. The majority of the tobacco smoked today is flue-cured, meaning, once harvested, the leaves are hung in custom-built barns and speed-dried by air from hot flues. Also known as "bright tobacco", because of its distinctive yellow colour, it is often blended with burley to make cigarette tobacco.

Why cigarettes?

Most tobacco goes to make cigarettes, which long ago outstripped pipe and cigar smoking and snuff as the favoured form of tobacco consumption. Britain and Ireland were among the first countries to take to cigarettes, which became the dominant method of tobacco use there in the aftermath of World War I; the same only happened in the US during World War II — later in most European countries.

The cigarette's popularity is largely due to developments in mass-production techniques. And like most consumable products today, industrialisation has meant the introduction of additives. Since 1970, up to 600 chemicals have been authorised for inclusion in tobacco, many of which are thought to enhance its carcinogenic powers.

They include: ammonia, which manufacturers insist is a flavouring, but critics say is added to increase the absorption of nicotine; propylene glycol, which manufacturers say is intended to moisten reconstituted tobacco (up to 30% of your cigarette), but health organisations say speeds the delivery of nicotine to the brain; and chocolate, which critics say is a sweetener added to make cigarettes palatable to children, but cigarette makers say is a flavouring (aren't those pretty much the same thing?).

The more aware you are of the presence of all these little extras, the more you should want to give up. But the more of them there are, the less likely you'll be able to. A middle ground could be to jack in the cigarettes (maybe you consider them expensive, maybe you're smoking too damn many, maybe you just think they're frightfully common, darling) and take up an alternative. There are many.

Shove it up your nostrils

It just might arouse some suspicion in public, inhaling a fingertip of powder through the nose. But what can anybody do? Snuff is legal. It's also a source of nicotine, it's not a cigarette, and you don't have to give some chemist a small fortune for the privilege of getting your hit. Snuff retails at about £1.20 a tin.

In 18th- and 19th-century Europe, snuff rivalled pipe-smoking as the most popular form of tobacco consumption. In Britain, it was the favoured method of consumption up until 1800, but in the 19th century was knocked off its perch by the pipe, which in turn was supplanted by the cigarette.

Although it can cause oral and nasal cancers, "snuffing" is not as dangerous as smoking. Derived from dark, fire-cured tobacco, it is now available in a variety of flavours and colours. The powder enjoyed something of a resurgence in 1990s' London, prompting Clive Bates, director of Action on Smoking and Health in the UK, to suggest changing the name of his organisation to Action on Snorting and Health. What a card.

A cigar is a smoke

Until recently, the popular image of a cigar lover was of a refined, appreciative, non-inhaling connoisseur, who liked to compare smoking a good cigar to going to bed with a beautiful woman and other such nonsense. Since high-end cigar smokers were rather few in number, it was unlikely you would meet anybody who might contradict this stereotype.

There was no shortage, though, of low-rent cigar smokers, whose ranks I still join occasionally. Every few months, having quit cigarettes, I buy a single Hamlet in the pub and inhale as fast as my little lungs can manage, to extract every molecule of nicotine. One cheap cigar per night quickly becomes ten, until I can stand the things no longer (no offence Mr Manufacturer, but they're not exactly Davidoffs old chap) and go back on cigarettes.

In recent times, however, cigar smoking has developed a middle-class. During the 1990s, as cigarette makers were dragged through the courts, the press, and the legislative chamber, luxury cigar sales tripled. Cigar bars and clubs opened across America and, increasingly, are appearing in Europe. From the covers of *Cigar Aficionado* magazine, launched in 1992 to capitalise on the growing trend for cigars, stared the likes of Arnold Schwarzenegger, Jack Nicholson,

James Woods, and a string of glamorous women (Sharon Stone, Demi Moore, Madonna), who have helped give cigars a softer image.

Documents from inside the cigar industry show these were the fruits of a plan first hatched in 1980 by the US Cigar Manufacturers' Association. There followed a media campaign involving product placement in movies, endorsements by celebrities and infiltration of the news media.

Despite these orchestrations that led to the cigar revival, I must confess to being in favour of them. For one thing, they are more healthful than cigarettes. If you stick to quality cigars, their high price means they can't be consumed in the kind of quantity that makes cigarettes so damaging. And, if ex-cigarette smokers can train themselves not to inhale, their throats, lungs and hearts suffer less. (Not inhaling isn't just a question of cigar manners. Cigar smoke is more alkaline than that from cigarettes, and dissolves more easily in saliva, so the nicotine dose is delivered without having to inhale the smoke into the lungs.)

Furthermore, while there is a complicated etiquette surrounding cigars, smokers should not let the air of exclusivity dissuade them from an otherwise enjoyable habit. Like wine in France or food in Italy, cigars are not a snob product in their countries of origin, Cuba and the Dominican Republic, but rather are enjoyed by all. Natives of these islands — and most people familiar with cigars — judge them individually for their taste and smoothness, rather than as characterless vehicles for a nicotine hit.

Fill up a pipe

It's hard to write of pipes without also mentioning dressing-gowns and slippers. With their *Dad's Army* image and small number of devotees (just 2% of British and Irish smokers take their tobacco through a pipe), pipes may have had their day.

But every smoke cloud has its silver lining. Like snuff, pipe tobacco is a lot cheaper than cigarettes. And while all that cleaning and filling may not be very appealing when you're dying for a smoke on your five-minute coffee break, at other times it has pleasant, ritualistic aspect to it. If you want to cut down, what better method than to introduce an element of inconvenience to your habit. And if few people smoke pipes, then at least they're different — stylish even. In a 2001 edition of the über-trendy *Wallpaper** magazine, a female model pulled on a white acrylic pipe made by a Netherlands company determined to lift pipe-smoking from the doldrums. Is the hour ripe for the return of the pipe? Could be, but ... oh I give up ... it's not very bloody likely.

Grow your own

It's not an alternative to smoking cigarettes but growing your own tobacco has its advantages. You will avoid the many chemicals which manufacturers add to cigarettes. As with any method that circumvents tobacco tax, it's a lot cheaper. And if smoking is suddenly outlawed, you'll have your personal supply.

The hard part is drying the tobacco to give it a pleasant taste. The cigarettes you buy in the shops are the result of hundreds of years of trial-and-error, and they contain all those additives which — evil and all as they are — stop your cigarettes tasting rotten.

For help, see **www.tobacco.org/Resources/lbguide.html#aa60**. You can buy seeds from **www.keepsmilin.com/tobacco.html**, and **www.seedman.com**, the site of UK-based gardener Alan Daly, offers guidance on planting and maintenance. You can join the Tilty Tobacco and Curing Co-operative, The Tily, Dunmow , Essex CM6-2EG, UK for £21. It sounds like a very respectable organisation (founded in 1948 by one Reverend Hugh Cuthbertson), and they'll send you a booklet called *Tobacco without Tears*.

That damned, elusive safe ciggie

In the futuristic film, *The Fifth Element,* Bruce Willis's character smokes a cigarette that is about 70% filter and 30% tobacco — the current proportions in reverse. It's possible. What's certain is that the cigarettes of the future will be less dangerous than those currently on the market.

Over the past 30 years, hundreds of patents have been filed for safer cigarettes, ranging from a catalytic converter to a little box to capture the smoke so that people around the smoker aren't affected. To date, few have gone beyond research stage, and none has been brought to market in any serious way.

But it looks like the tobacco firms may have changed their minds about a healthier alternative. British American Tobacco has been taking an interest in the work of a company called Star Scientific, which has developed a tobacco low in "nitrosamines", thought to be the main cancer-causing agents in tobacco. And RJ Reynolds, which abandoned its smokeless cigarette, Premier, after smokers in trials said it tasted "like a fart", is now testing its successor, Eclipse.

These two products give us a glimpse into the future of the cigarette. In time, the cigarette could become less like a cigarette and more like the nicotine inhalers already available down at your local chemists. So that's what you have to look forward to.

I say "you", because none of this is relevant to me any more. I'm giving up tomorrow. Monday at the latest.

Acknowledgements

Many, many thanks to Faith O'Grady of the Lisa Richards Agency, for taking on this book and finding the right publisher. Merçi, Michael McCarthy, illustrator, and Jon Berkeley, cover designer. Mille grazie to Hugh Linehan, David Porter and Ann-Marie Power, for their advice and encouragement. Danke schön especially to Ciara Considine and Anthony Glavin, the editors, Edwin Higel, the publisher, and everybody else at New Island Books. Finally, gurrameelamohaguth to Niamh, for her love, support, editorial eye and innumerable cups of tea.